SWAMP TOWN

SWAMP TOWN

JAMES P. DANIELS

TATE PUBLISHING
AND ENTERPRISES, LLC

Published by Tate Publishing & Enterprises, LLC
127 E. Trade Center Terrace | Mustang, Oklahoma 73064 USA
1.888.361.9473 | www.tatepublishing.com

Tate Publishing is committed to excellence in the publishing industry. The company reflects the philosophy established by the founders, based on Psalm 68:11,
"The Lord gave the word and great was the company of those who published it."

Book design copyright © 2015 by Tate Publishing, LLC. All rights reserved.
Cover design by Rtor Maghuyop
Interior design by Jimmy Sevilleno

Published in the United States of America

ISBN: 978-1-68028-357-0
Fiction / African American / General
15.01.29

CHAPTER I

IT WAS THE fall of 1918 in the south of France. A squad of black American soldiers were camped a few miles from the war zone. Sgt. David Bradley was in charge of the third squad and wanted to make a name for himself.

A soldier, whose name was Bert Benson, found it hard to follow the sergeant's orders and that created a problem for the two of them.

Bert was born in 1892. He was drafted in the US Army in 1916 and served his country in England, Belgium, and France. Bert was a tall black man, who stood about six feet two inches. His muscular build was the result of the hard work that he had to do while working on a farm in the south of Louisiana. He was always neatly dressed and ready for any task that his sergeant had for him.

The treatment of the black military men in those days was horrible and he had his share of problems. But that morning, the sergeant had no reason to attack him.

It was a cold rainy morning in the south of France, and Bert was ill with the flu. The sergeant had been pushing the squad pretty hard and he accused Bert of faking it and insisted that Bert continued the five-mile march that they had to do before breakfast. When they return to their tents after the march was completed, Bert went inside his tent to get dry cloths and a dry towel to dry himself off. He was soaked from the rain and the sweat which was caused by such a long march but this was no concern for the sergeant. So when the sergeant saw him coming out of the tent, he was upset that Bert had left his post, so he walked up behind him and struck him on the head with an ax handle.

When Bert woke up two days later, he found himself in the hospital with his head wrapped with bandages. His buddy, who grew up with him, was sitting at his bedside, crying with Bert's food tray in his lap, while his tears, sweat, and mucus dropped into it. Bert looked into his friend's eyes and saw the tears running down his cheeks and felt the hurt in his friend's heart. He promised his friend that some day, he would get even.

"Don't worry," his friend told him. "You just concentrate on getting well now."

Bert was in the hospital for two weeks, but it was two months before he got back into action.

One day, his friend came to him and told him that he had seen the sergeant going through the woods toward a house where some French women were known to hang out. Knowing that this was his chance to get even, Bert made his plans to catch the sergeant alone. Before leaving his tent, Bert located the ax handle under his friend's bed where his friend had hid it. The weapon had been kept there for three months, waiting for Bert. Bert took the ax handle and went out the back door of the tent. From there, he took a shortcut through the woods and caught up with the sergeant just before he got to his destination. He ambushed the sergeant from his hiding place behind a bush and left him lying there.

The sergeant was found lying in the grass by the side of the road. The final report said that the sergeant was last seen going down into the woods. It was never known what had happened to the sergeant. Some said that he may have been killed by a sniper or maybe he got lost. No one officially said anything.

The outfit was getting ready to break camp and head back home, and one missing black man was not important enough for the military to be concerned with. A few weeks later, Bert and his friend were transferred to an army camp in Arkansas, and when Bert was discharged, he moved to Baton Rouge, Louisiana.

Bert's father was the son of a slave and had moved to Swamp Town and worked for a man named Williams as a tenant farmer. Mr. Williams owned all of the land in and around Swamp Town, which was a small hamlet somewhere between the Mississippi River and Lake Pontchartrain in the state of Louisiana. The neighborhood was formerly a slave plantation but now it was inhabited by the people who once lived in these huts that had been used as slave quarters just a few years earlier.

Bert had moved back to the Williams's farm and worked with his father as a tenant farmer. After his father died, Bert took his father's place and later married his wife Sarah. Sarah was a beautiful woman. She stood about five feet nine inches tall with greenish brown eyes. The tint in her eyes and the caramel color of her skin exposed the mixture of her racial makeup. They lived in the house that had been used by the slave overseer. This house was a bit larger than the other houses of Swamp Town and was surrounded by pasture and barns that housed the animals and most of the tools and equipment used on the plantation.

All the houses were located near a bayou with a slow flowing creek. This creek was beautiful with a deep area on the south side while the north side was shallow and full of swampy plants. There were a ray of flowers—orchids, Venus flytraps, and cattails—above the water level, while lily pads lay in the shallow waters with large white flowers. The creek flowed from the Mississippi River east to Lake Pontchartrain.

At the end of the Civil War, former slaves were supposed to have received forty acres and a mule. That never happened so they were left to work as sharecroppers with the man who had previously owned them as slaves. As sharecroppers, a situation was created where they did the work and the landowner supplies the land, equipment, and supplies and the profits were to be divided equally at the end of the harvest. However, it was hard to tell what your share was when the landowner is the only one who keeps records. When you are left with nothing you must decide on how to survive and sharecropping was the only thing they had left.

Bert was now tending the farm of his father's landowner and receiving just enough to keep himself and his family alive. All the property on the farm, including the livestock, belonged to the landowner. Bert had to get permission from the landowner to slaughter even the chickens or ducks for food.

Bert had great skills in hunting and fishing, and with so much wild this game around, there was plenty of meat for the family. He hunted rabbits, nutrias, and raccoons, and the fishing was great.

It was five o'clock in the morning and time for Bert to get up. Part of his job was to get up early, go to the barn, and feed the animals before he had his breakfast. This morning, Bert did as he often does after feeding the animals. He climbed up on the top rail of the fence facing east into the rising sun. It was always a beautiful sight and this morning was no different. This was a beautiful place and a person could even get used to the smell of the stables and the musk permeating from the swamp.

The area was filled with life. There was always the sound of animals scurrying about. Birds were chirping and frogs croaking. As he sat there on the fence, a rooster flew to the top of a post a few feet from him and gave his morning call, inviting everyone to wake up to a new day. This was Bert's notice so he climbed down from the fence and started walking back to the house for his breakfast.

Bert and Sarah had not talked much with each other for about two weeks now, not since she had come into the house seeming to be upset. He had asked her what the problem was and she had mumbled saying everything was going to be okay.

Approaching the house, he wondered about the problem but decided not to press the issue. The smell of fried bacon, eggs, and sliced sweet potatoes sprinkled with nutmeg, met him as he entered the kitchen door.

"Come in," she said. "Your breakfast is ready."

Bert walked in quietly and sat down at the table, he looked at Sarah and said, "I know that something is bothering you, but we don't have to talk about it until you are ready."

"Thank you," Sarah said quietly.

The plantation crops consisted of corn, soybean, cotton, and a bit of rice in a few areas. After breakfast, Bert walked back to the barn yard, went into the barn, and got the mule's bridle. He put it on the mule and hooked the mule up to the cart. He then put his plow and gear on the cart and headed off to the field.

As he rode past the house, Sarah was standing at the door when she called out to him.

"I'll be working in the cornfield with Cora and Mable," she said.

"Do you want me to pick you up after work?" he asked.

"No, I'll walk home with the girls."

"Okay. Have a good day," said Bert. With that, he headed toward the cotton field.

Sarah's regular job was working in the landowner's house, but she had been laid off. She had been told by Mrs. Williams that she was not to return to the landowner's house until a month after the incident had passed, and that she was going to ask Fanny, wife of one of her tenant farmers, to work in her place until then.

After Bert left, she went back into the house, cleaned up the kitchen, and then walked down to the cornfield to meet Cora and Mable.

The cotton field was about a mile away from Bert's house. On the way, Bert saw Ray Jones and his sons, Ben and Ray Jr., who were walking down the path that led to the main road. and approached them.

"Whoa," Bert said to the mule. As he stopped, he called to Ray and the boys. "You guys need a ride?" he asked.

"Yes," Ray said. "I'm going to be in the field right next to your cotton field."

"Hop in," Bert said.

Ray climbed into the cart and sat on the bench beside Bert. The two boys sat in the rear of the cart, with their feet hanging down, swinging back and forward in the cool morning air.

Ray noticed that Bert was unusually quiet. Bert had not said anything since they had gotten into the cart.

"Are you okay?" Ray asked.

Looking straight ahead as if no one was there but him, Bert said, "There is something wrong in my house. I have asked her what the problem is, but she won't say."

Ray kept quiet.

Ben and Ray Jr. had their fishing rods with them and as they rode along the road; they were practicing their casting. Sometimes, their lines would get tangled in the weeds and they would have to jump out of the cart to untangle their lines and then run back to catch up to the cart. Meanwhile, Bert continued his silence for the rest of the trip to the cotton field.

When they got to the cotton field, Ray said, "We'll get off here." Then he turned to his friend. "Now, Bert, don't you worry too much. Everything is going to be all right."

"I hear you." Bert mumbled, but he was worried and depressed about what was going on in his house. Now he had to get some work done so he hitched his mule to the plow and went to his field and started plowing his cotton.

Sarah was in the field with Cora and Mable. These two field hands had been working in these fields all their lives. They were two dark-skinned ladies who were wearing full-length, full-bodied skirts. They had on loose fitting tops and a scarf covering their hair. This way of dressing was used mostly for keeping their bodies cool and the dust out of their hair. Both women were tall and statuesque, reminding all who saw them of the proud Mandingo people of West Africa.

Sarah was working with them, but her mind was not on what she was supposed to be doing. She had to find a way to tell Bert what her problem was but the time was not right, not yet. The other women could see that Sarah was not in much of a mood for talking, so they left her alone.

Bert ended his day at five o'clock and went by the field where Ray had been working, but Ray and the boys had already quit for the day. Ray had decided to leave Bert to his misery and left a little early so the boys decided to go down to the creek to do a little fishing. It was a nice day so Ray took a nice quiet walk home alone.

On his way home, Bert saw the two boys fishing at a familiar spot and decided to stop and see if Ray was there.

"You guys catching anything?" Bert yelled out.

"I caught a cat," Ray Jr. said.

"I caught two sunfish and a turtle," Ben added.

"Is your father over there?" Bert asked.

"No," Ray Jr. said. "He told us to tell you that he had gone home."

"Okay," said Bert. "I'll see you guys tomorrow."

It had been almost a month since Mrs. Williams had asked Sarah not to return to work. She was working in the field with Cora and Mable when Fanny, the lady who had taken Sarah's place at the big house, stopped by on her way home from the Williams's house.

"How are you ladies doing?" Fanny asked as she approached them. Fanny was wearing a neatly pressed black dress that hugged her body in all the right places; her white apron was starched and ironed smoothly and tied with a large bow in the back. Her hair had been pressed and combed back and formed into a ponytail with a white bow holding it in place.

"I'm fine." Cora smiled. "How have you been doing? I see that you are still working up there in the big house?"

Mable laughed and said, "I bet she's doing better than we are out here in all this heat."

"I'm doing just fine," said Fanny. "How are you ladies doing?" Fanny walked over to Sarah and asked, "What about you, Sarah? Are you doing okay?"

"I'm okay," Sarah replied quietly, not really wanting to talk.

"Mrs. Williams told me to tell you to report to work on Monday," Fanny told Sarah.

"Thanks," Sarah said quietly. "This was good news." It made her feel better but jittery, not knowing how she would be received back at the big house.

As Fanny walked away, she turned and said to the other two girls, "I'll be back out here with you two on Monday."

Except for the nervousness, Sarah was happy to get back to work at the Williams's house. There were lots of work, cooking, and cleaning this big house, but it was a clean, comfortable environment and Mrs. Williams was easy to work for.

After Bert left for work that Monday morning, Sarah took special care in dressing for work. She made sure that her clothes were exceptionally clean and well pressed. She had to walk about a mile to get to the big house which sat up on a hill overlooking the five thousand acres of land which included the hamlet of Swamp Town.

The north side of the property was bordered by the creek. Beyond the creek, the swamp extended for a mile or so with the water level at an average depth of about two feet. The roots of old dead cypress trees and water lilies were scattered though out the area, with the exception of the south side which had some places with eight to ten feet of water and a host of other plants that grew in southern Louisiana.

When Sarah got to the house, she found the key in the location where she normally kept it. She entered the house and went to work preparing breakfast for the Williams.

Robert Williams, a big man who stood about six feet two inches with black hair that was beginning to turn gray around the edges, was a busy man who always dressed well. He was the first to smell the aroma of the smoked ham permeating throughout the house. He knew that Sarah was back and she was preparing his favorite breakfast. Along with the ham, she made fried eggs, grits, and hot rolls with molasses.

Mr. Williams was the first to get up, take his bath, and was seated at the table when Mrs. Williams arrived.

"Good morning," Mrs. Williams said. "I'm glad you're back, Sarah."

"Good morning," Sarah said. "I'm happy to be back."

After Mr. Williams had finish his breakfast, he walked over to Sarah, looked into her eyes and whispered as if he didn't want anyone to hear. "I'm so happy that you're back. No one can cook a breakfast like you can."

Mr. Williams worked at the parish seat in Baton Rouge and only went out on the farm to make sure that the crops were being cultivated as they should be. The sharecroppers had worked the land all their lives. They knew what they were doing and was happy that they were left for alone most of the time.

Mr. Williams went back to his seat and poured himself a second cup of coffee. "What field is Bert working on today?" he asked Sarah.

"He's plowing the cotton on the east end," Sarah replied.

Mr. Williams stood up. "I'll be on the east end with Bert. Then I'm going to see what the other tenants are doing."

Mrs. Williams was a stately woman with natural red hair. She stood about five feet eleven inches tall and was always well dressed and never without full makeup. After her husband had left the house, she came in and complimented Sarah on such a fine breakfast. "I want you to know that Robert Jr. has returned to school, so there will be no need to cook or clean for him," she told Sarah.

"Will he be back?" Sarah asked.

"Not regularly," Mrs. Williams replied quietly. "I hope that he get a job and get his own place in Baton Rouge." Mrs. Williams paused, then said, "By the way, did you talk to Bert?" Mrs. Williams asked.

Softly, Sarah replied, "No, not yet."

"Give it a little more time," Mrs. Williams said.

Bert could see the dust from Mr. Williams's Model T Ford heading down the long and dusty road toward him. The two spent the entire morning checking all the crops that Bert was responsible for. When Mr. Williams left, he was pleased with Bert's work. Bert felt relaxed and after completing the field that he was working in, he decided to take a break and do a little fishing.

Bert kept a fishing rod in his cart. There was some good fishing where his friend Ray's sons Ben and Ray Jr. were fishing a few days ago and that's where Bert kept a small dingy tied to a cypress tree. After digging a few worms and catching a few grasshoppers, Bert climbed into his dingy and rowed out into an area where he knew that he could catch his supper. His favorite spot was where the lily pads nearly covered the surface of the water and while casting his bait where the big fish waited in the coolness of the shade and sitting there in his dingy. He was more relaxed than he had been in a long time.

It was not long before he felt a tug on his line.

As he leaned back, he grunted. He could feel his line jiggle at the tip. "This is a big one," Bert said to himself. "There is going to be some good eating tonight." The big catfish struggled to free himself but Bret continued to reel in his supper. *That's a good one,* he thought as he was leaning back in his dingy and pulling that big boy in the boat.

Bert continued fishing for the rest of the afternoon, catching four nice sunfish and two smaller catfish.

When Bert got home, he unhooked the mule, put away the gear, and cleaned the fish. He had had a very nice relaxing day. He sat there for a few minutes, feeding the heads of the fish to the cat. Not wanting to get to the house and find Sarah starting to cook something else, he figured he had better go into the house before she got there. When Sarah got home, she entered the front door just as Bert entered the back door.

She heard him yell, "Sarah, I've got some fish for dinner."

"Oh, good," she replied. "Hope you cleaned them. I had to work kind of hard today, but it was nice to get back to work at the big house."

"Yeah, they are clean," he replied.

While she was cooking the food, Bert went outside and sat down on a bench on the front porch. Reaching into the pocket of his bib overalls, he pulled out a bag of smoking tobacco and rolled himself a cigarette; relaxing there, leaning with his back against the wall of the porch, having himself a good smoke. As he sat there inhaling the smoke, he thought, *It had been a very nice day.* He could smell fish and corn bread fritters frying, and she had put on a pot of collard greens with ham hocks.

After Sarah had finished cooking, she came to the front door and said, "Bert, your food is ready." Then she turned and went back into the kitchen. After they had eaten, Bert went back to his bench on the porch. A few minutes later, Sarah came out on the porch carrying a chair. She placed the chair next to the bench and sat down beside him. She looked at Bert and smiled— a smile that Bert had not seen since the incident. "Bert, you don't have to sleep in the front room any longer…if you don't want to." The smile lingered there for a few seconds, saying just what Bert wanted to hear.

Bert had not slept with her since the incident and having had a very nice day, so far, he could see no reason to spoil such a blissful ending to such a blissful day.

Things went very well between them for a month or so, until one day she came to him and told him that she was pregnant. After that, she went back into her shell. Bert's thoughts of Sarah confused and depressed him so much so that after he worked until 2:00 p.m. that next Saturday and then taking care of the animals, he decided to go for a walk down to Jessie Mae's place and have himself a strong one. Jessie Mae ran the juke joint a mile or so from Bert's house. He just wanted to get away for a while and Jesse's juke joint was just the place to do it.

When he entered the joint, he went to the back of the room and motioned for Jesse Mae to bring him a drink. She poured him a shot of corn whiskey and a glass of lemonade. Bert sat there with a shot of corn whiskey, chasing it with lemonade. He was alone now in the place that he wanted to be, listening to the music that he wanted to hear, trying to calm the thoughts in his mind.

The joint was a small room, about thirty feet by thirty feet with a lean-to shed at the back. Inside the place was a bar and three small tables. Bert sat alone at the table in the corner furthest from the bar. Two other patrons were in the bar talking to Jessie Mae. When she saw that Bert needed another shot of corn whiskey, she came over and placed it on the table.

One of the guys, who was sitting at the bar, had just ordered his third drink, said to Jesse Mae, "Who does that guy think he is? Can't he come to the bar like the rest of us?"

"Don't you worry about it," Jessie snapped. "This is my place and I'll serve people when and where I please. Just relax and enjoy yourself," she said with a smile.

Jessie was five feet two inches tall. She wore skirts most of the time with a two-inch-wide belt that put emphasis on the petite waistline and highlighted the curves above it. She wore her hair short and straight with a part on the left side. She was a beautiful woman who had returned to Swamp Town from the city of Chicago.

Unfazed, the man said, "I'm going over there and find out why he's so special."

"Don't do that," Jessie said without a smile.

"Why not?" asked the man.

Jesse said as she wiped the table, "Because I don't want him to kill you." She continued to wipe the countertop, then she said, "Sometimes, it's better to leave a quiet man alone."

The man thought better about his action and went back to his seat. Jesse Mae gave the man a couple of nickels and said to the man, "Play us a couple of nice tunes."

The man walked over to the juke box and dropped the coins into the juke box, then came back to his seat and relaxed for the rest of the evening.

Around six o'clock, Jesse's son came into the bar. He heated up the stove and started preparing some food for the night. That evening, they had fried chicken, buttered biscuits, collard greens, and sweet Kool-Aid on the menu.

At seven thirty, a wagon on which three musicians were playing music, approached the place. A drummer, a sax player, and a guitar player all climbed out of the wagon and set their equipments up to play right beside Bert's table. They started off playing the blues. Bert had not intended to stay so long but the blues were just what Bert needed. As the music played, more people began entering the joint. The place was now getting a bit too crowded for him so Bert had one more shot of corn whiskey and decided that it was time for him to go home.

Seeing that Bert was ready to leave, Jessie Mae went over to his table and sat down. She looked into Bert's eyes with a smile and whispered, "If you and I were still together, you wouldn't be sitting over here with such a sad look."

"Jessie Mae," Bert said, "if we had stayed together, one of us would be dead by now."

"Yeah," she said with a hearty laugh. "But we had some great times, didn't we?"

He looked at her and gave a knowing smile. Even though they were not together anymore, they were still good friends.

Jessie Mae then called her son and told him to make sure that Bert got home safely. Jesse's son, a big boy, about seventeen years old, walked Bert all the way to his yard and watched him as he got to his porch and sat on his favorite bench.

It was midsummer.

Bert was up and headed out to the barn to feed the animals. On the west side of the barn, he had a hogpen with ten grown hogs; two of which had young pigs. As he left the house, he heard the barking of dogs and distressed sounds from the hogs. He rushed back into the house, got his shotgun, and rushed to the hogpen. By the time he got there, the dogs had already killed four pigs and were still attacking the hogs.

Bert fired a shot from one barrel, killing one dog. The second dog had the mother of the pigs by her throat. Bert got down on one knee to get a better shot. The dog released the hog and turned to charge Bert as he placed a shell into the second barrel of the shotgun and pulled both triggers. The sound rang out, the buckshots struck the dog just as he leaped for Bert's throat. The dog fell to the ground like a sack of guts. By that time, the third dog took off across the field. There was not enough time for another shot so he put his gun away and went to work.

Two days later, Bert was approached in his corn field by two white men. One of them said that he had been told that Bert had killed his dog. Bert admitted that he had killed the dogs because they had killed the hogs and that they should not have been on the property. This angered the men and one of them shouted.

"I ought to kill you right here and right now," the man said. The other man also yelled out obscenities at Bert.

"But they were killing the hogs…" Bert pleaded.

"I don't give a damn what they did. I should hang you right now." said the man. His eyes were lit up with rage and he pointed his shotgun at Bert.

"No, no," the man's partner said. "We'll make him pay for them."

He turned to his friend and said, "You know these dogs are worth fifty dollars each, you know, a hundred dollars is worth a lot more than a dead nigger."

"Where is he going to get a hundred dollars?" the other man asked.

"I don't give a damn," the man said, then he turned to Bert with a hard look. "We will be at your house at two o'clock Saturday, and you'd better have my money."

Bert had no idea what to do. That afternoon, he walked down to Jessie's place and told her what had happened. The thought of her friend being in danger put her in a fighting mode. She spoke of getting her friends together and meeting the KKK at Bert's house for a showdown, but Bert had to calm her down. "That will just get a bunch of people killed," he said. "I'm going to Mr. Williams's house and ask him if he will loan me the money."

Bert went to the Williams's home, but Mr. Williams was not there. He explained to Mrs. Williams what had happened. "Wait there on the porch until Mr. Williams gets home. He will take care of all of this mess," Mrs. Williams said.

Bert sat there for about two hours until off in a distance he could see the dust of Mr. Williams's car coming down the road. As he drove up, Mr. Williams wondered. What is Bert doing here? Did a mule die? Did Bert bust up a plow on a stump or something? "Whatever it was, it'll have to wait until tomorrow," he said to himself. As Mr. Williams was getting out of his car, he asked Bert what he was doing there and what he wanted.

Bert stood up and walked down to meet Mr. Williams. He told him in detail what had happened and that he needed to borrow one hundred dollars or the men said that they would kill him.

"I'll take care this." Mr. Williams sighed. "I'll be there tomorrow at two o'clock."

At one thirty the next day, Bert asked Sarah to walk down to Ray Jones's house. At one forty-five, he picked up his shotgun and walked out on his front porch and sat down on his bench. He heard himself saying, "I just don't feel like being hung today." *So if they hang me, they will just say another black man was hung today. But if I kill two of them, they will say that a black man killed two before he was hung today. Now that sounds a lot better,* he thought. At that point, he found himself calmly sitting there waiting and wishing for two o'clock to hurry up and get there.

At two o'clock, three men drove up to his front yard. The driver got out of the car and started walking up to the house with a shotgun in his hand. Bert thought, *I might just have to kill one. The other two may just drive off.* He picked up his shotgun and quietly put two shells in the chamber. The man hesitated and lowered his weapon. Still he asked, "Where is my money?" Quietly, Bert replied, "I don't have it." He rubbed the gun barrel and added, "I don't feel like hanging today."

Sarah was sitting in Ray Jones's house with the whole family. They were as quiet as could be, waiting for the sound of gunfire. On their left, they could hear a car approaching. Mr. Williams drove up to Bert's place and got out of his car, yelling at the top of his voice, "What the hell's going on here?"

The man glared at Bert while yelling, "This boy killed my dogs."

Bert just stood there never moving a muscle.

"Did you know that the dogs were killing hogs?" Mr. Williams asked.

"I don't care about the damn hogs!" the man shouted out.

Mr. Williams looked at Bert, then turned to the man. "Do you care about dying?" he asked the man, who stood there with a blank look on his face.

"Take a good look at that man's face, boys," Mr. Williams said.

The men stared at Bert's face. Mr. Williams then turned and said, "Do you see that? Do you see what I see? He don't care about dying, boys. He's already been to hell. He's just thinking of taking someone with him this time."

Mr. Williams approached the man and said quietly, "The hogs belong to me, and I pay him to take care of my animals. Now," he lowered his head. "Your dogs killed five hundred dollars' worth of hogs and he killed one hundred dollars' worth of dogs." Then he stared at the man and said, "How do you want to handle this?"

The man said nothing.

The men watched as Mr. Williams walked back to his car and returned with a Colt .45, which he handed to Bert. "This is the present that I promised you," he said.

The men looked at Mr. Williams, knowing that he gave Bert the handgun in front of them to protect himself if they tried something later in the cornfield.

Mr. Williams said to the men, "I guess you should know that Bert spent three years in France fighting the Germans."

With that, the man backed slowly away, got in their car and left.

Mr. Williams softly smiled. "You know, Bert, I think we should kill one of those hogs and have us a big barbecue."

"Let me know when you are ready," Bert replied.

As he got back into his car, he gave Bert a once over. "Okay, I will," Mr. Williams said.

Bert turned and walked back into the house.

Mr. Williams stopped at Ray Jones's house and told Ray to tell Sarah that Bert was okay. He looked down then looked back at Ray and said, "That Bert...he is one hell of a man."

When Sarah heard this news, she ran out of the house and went home to Bert.

Bert felt a bit nervous going out into the fields after the conflict with the KKK. He would often take the gift that Mr. Williams had given him to work, keeping it in his belt, under his overalls, because he expected the KKK to show up at any time but they never did. Maybe it was because Mr. Williams had paid them or maybe it was because of the present that Mr. Williams had given Bert in front of them. He never found out.

Three weeks later, Bert checked with Mr. Williams and made plans for the barbecue in midsummer. All of the people in and around Swamp Town were invited. Bert went to Jessie Mae's place to make arrangements for some of her famous grape wine, which was a mixture of 80 percent wine and 20 percent corn whiskey. It was a good time to have a barbecue. Watermelons and cantaloupes were ripe and sweet corn was ready to be picked. Bert had the Jones boys clean out the barbeque pit that had been used two years earlier. The grate was still in the barn and there was plenty of hickory wood left.

Sarah asked Fanny and Jessie Mae to help her with the Kool-Aid lemonade and vegetables. Sadie Jones prepared the potato salad and Jessie Mae delivered a mason jar of her wine the evening the hog was killed. Bert, Ray, and his boys loaded the hog on the grate and relaxed while the hog was slowly cooked for ten hours. The aroma of the barbecue cooking covered the entire area and people came by checking out the progress of the pig thoughout the night.

The barbecue started at two o'clock. People came from throughout the area bringing their specialties of foods and oddities of items that would help the host in any way they could.

A Creole cousin of Sarah showed up with a big pot of gumbo. Jessie Mae brought the band who had played at her bar. They got out of their wagon by the side of the road and started playing as they walked toward the aroma of the freshly cooked chopped barbecue and melons.

Over the still hot pit, there had been placed a sheet of tin and wet burlap bags which was covered with a bushels of freshly picked corn. The corn was topped with more wet burlap bags. This method of cooking steamed the corn inside the husk making the corn sweet and delicious.

Mr. Williams showed up with two families of white sharecroppers who happily joined in with the feasting and merriment.

Mr. Williams walked over to Sarah and said quietly, "Mrs. Williams asked me to ask you to send her a plate of BBQ."

Sarah gave a little chuckle. "I will," she said. "I'll get it when you are ready to leave, just give me a nod."

The band had gotten set up and was playing the most up-to-date music. They played "Blueberry Hill," "Bad, Bad Whiskey," and "Sweet Georgia Brown." People had come from miles around. There was singing and dancing by the old and the young. Some of the young ones tried their luck at doing the limbo. There was plenty of food for everyone and laughter was heard throughout the area.

As daylight started fading, the crowd started thinning out. The barbecue was winding down and Sarah had started to take the dishes into the house. While helping with the dishes, Jessie entered the kitchen and saw Sarah sitting at the table.

"What's the matter?" Jessie asked. Jessie was concerned and wanted to know what was wrong with her friend.

Sarah slowly shook her head. "I just can't get myself together," she whispered.

"I know you and Bert have had some troubles, but it can't be that bad." Jesse touched her hand. "He says that you want talk to him," Jesse continued.

Sarah rubbed her wrists. "I can't. I don't know how," she said.

Jessie glanced at Sarah's belly. "You two must be doing something. I can see the results in your stomach. Have you told him yet?" she asked?

Sarah touched her growing belly softly. "I can't. I don't know how to tell him this."

Jessie stood up and said, "You will have to tell him some time." Then she went out the door in silence.

It was getting late and all of the men who lived in Swamp Town had gotten together to help Bert clean up the trash. It had been a good day. There was plenty to eat and no one had caused any trouble. The Jones boys and two of their sisters were still singing hymns outside, and Sarah had prepared a large feast for Mrs. Williams which included barbecue, a bowl of gumbo, steamed corn, and a quart of Jesse's grape wine was ready for Mr. Williams to take with him.

Mrs. Williams had smelled the barbecue before Mr. Williams had gotten to the door. He took the food to the kitchen, placed it on the table, and joined his wife, eating another meal for himself. After enjoying a delicious meal, Mrs. Williams told her husband, "I got a letter from your son today."

Their son, Robert Jr., a carbon copy of his father, had been out of the house for more than five months. He had said that he was going back to college to complete his education. Mr. Williams reached for a napkin and asked, "Has he signed up for classes yet?" as he wiped his lips.

Mrs. Williams did not look at her husband but said, "He says that he is going to sign up for fall classes."

"What's his major?" Mr. Williams asked.

"I don't know," Mrs. Williams began to tap her fingers on the table. "He says that he has an apartment in Baton Rouge."

Mr. Williams rose from the table and said, "When you write him, tell him to try to get a job."

CHAPTER 2

ROBERT JR. HAD gone by the college, but he had not tried to sign up for class. He spent most of his time in bars looking for girls and had met some of his friends from the year he dropped out of class. His friends Tommy Shelton and Bob Walker had not dropped out of school just yet, but they had not been studying either.

Tommy and Bob were out of school for the summer and had talked Robert Jr. into going to New Orleans for a bit of fun. Tommy's father was a dealer in cotton and corn. He was from old money and there was plenty of it.

Tommy was a fancy dresser, wearing high class clothes with expensive Italian shoes and Panama hats. He was six feet tall with blond hair and weighed about 180 pounds. He drove a fancy car with a rumble seat in the rear. Bob tried to dress as well as

Tommy but could not compete because his bank account would not allow him to do so.

Bob was a bit shorter, with brown hair, weighing about 165, and was always trying to impress the other two guys. Robert Jr. was using the money that his mother had given him for school to keep him going for a while, but at the rate that he was spending it, he would surely run out soon. He seldom hesitated to buy drinks for his friends and even their associates. The three of them got together a week after they met at school and headed off to New Orleans. Their first and most important priority was to find themselves a place to live and they found themselves a three-room flat, two blocks off Bourbon Street in New Orleans.

New Orleans was a party town and they were not used to this much excitement. There was dining and dancing from midday until late at night. The waitresses wore scantily dressed clothes and served strong drinks, and this was the type of place that they were looking for.

Instead of attending school, they spent most of their time in bars. It was the lack of money on Bob's behalf that caused the three of them to slow down. Robert Jr. sobered up for a few days and decided to go down to the Gulf Coast and relax for a while. He found himself sitting on the dock admiring the shrimp boats. He was amazed at their size and at how many shrimp they brought in from the Gulf.

One day, while sitting at the dock watching the boats come in, he noticed one boat with two mates—one of which was a young Creole girl. He thought if she can do this job, so could he. With no hesitation, he went over and asked the captain if he needed any help on his boat.

The captain gave Robert the once over and said, "Yes, but do you think you can handle it?" he asked.

"I'll give it a good try," said Robert, looking the captain in the eye, trying to impress him.

The captain told Robert Jr. that he would have to report for work at four in the morning. "Do you think that you can make that time?" he asked.

"I'll be here," Robert replied.

When he left the dock, he walked past a fish stand and there was the girl who he had just seen getting off the boat. He stopped. "I thought I just saw you getting of a shrimp boat," he said to her.

The young girl seemed unimpressed and said to him, "Yeah, it was me. You were talking to my father." Then she added. "Sometimes I help him when he's shorthanded." She offered her hand. "By the way, I'm Marge."

"I'm Robert. Your father asked me to report for work tomorrow."

Marge waved and strolled away. She had Robert's attention.

Robert returned to his flat and told his friends that he had gotten a job working on a shrimp boat.

They were not pleased.

"What did you do that for?" said Bob, who was lying on the couch. He was irritated at Robert for breaking up the group. "I thought we were going back to Baton Rouge?"

"What's the problem?" Robert asked. "I'm just going to work until the end of the season." He didn't understand the tension in their voices. Then he replied, "I'm going back and sign up for classes myself."

Bob sat up. "Well, we are going back to Baton Rouge. You can do what you want."

"I have money to last me for a while and I'll be getting paid," Robert said.

Bob was firm. "We're going back, I want to leave tomorrow."

"Fine with me," Tommy agreed.

Robert was done with the conversation. "Don't worry about me," Robert told them. "I'll be okay."

Robert was up early the next morning. He walked the four blocks down to the dock and met the boat captain.

Paul Lowe. The captain was a lean, weather-beaten man. His boat was his world and he was in charge of his world. The first mate was a black man, small in stature, but seemed to anticipate the captain's orders before the captain gave them. He had been working with Captain Lowe for about ten years. His name was Pete Sampson.

The captain gave Robert instructions on what his duties were and how they were to be carried out. This morning, they headed southwest to a place where he expected to find plenty of large shrimp. When they reached their destination, as they let out the nets, Robert was on one side and Pete on the other. Robert was not used to this kind of work so he was lagging behind. This was also his first time working with a black man as an equal. Instead of Robert trying to keep up with Pete, he started trying to tell Pete to keep up with him and this created a problem.

Captain Lowe was surprised that Robert was having a problem working with Pete, so he went to his new guy and told him that he had to get in the rhythm with Pete. His manner was gruff. The net had to go out evenly and the young man had to pay attention to the moves of his first mate. Robert felt that Pete should be trying to keep up with him but said nothing. He had not expected to be working side by side with a black man, but he had to try since his friends had gone back to Baton Rouge and he needed the money to pay for his rent.

When they docked that evening, Captain Lowe felt Robert needed a reality check. As he walked the deck, he said with a straight face, "Pete has worked with me for ten years, and I have never had a complaint. You got a problem working on equal terms with a black man?" he questioned Robert.

Robert was shocked. "The black people that I know always worked for us," he replied.

The captain shook his head at the young man's ignorance. "Out here on the water," he said with a hard look. "We all have to work together. Each man must hold his own at all times and be ready to assist his partner if needed."

When Robert left the dock that evening, he was worn out. He had never worked so hard in his life and almost walked past the fish stand where Marge was working.

"How did the day go?" she called out as he nearly passed her.

He dragged his body back to the stand and said, "I'm a little tired but I'll be okay."

Marge was trying to size Robert up. "I'm about ready to close up. You want to have a drink?"

"Yes, where are we going?" Robert was suddenly no longer tired.

"Just up the street. It's a nice place and you can get a sandwich there if you are hungry."

He was too tired to eat, but since Marge had suggested it, he told her, "That's a good idea."

Marge went back to closing the stand. "So how did you like working with my father?" she asked.

Robert sat heavily on a bench beside the stand. "He's okay, I guess. I'll just have to get used to working with a black man."

Marge stopped. "You mean Pete? He's one of the nicest men I know. You'll get used to him. Just think of him as a friend instead of a black man."

"I'll give it a try."

After she secured her stand, the two of them walked up the street to a bar called The Red Rooster. The customers were mostly fishermen from the area and Marge knew them all. When they walked into the bar, all the men turned and greeted the two of them, all the while trying to see who the stranger was with her.

"Guys," Marge said to her friends, "this is Robert. He is working with my father."

The men all nodded.

Robert and Marge walked over to the bar and sat down. "I'll have a bourbon," Marge said.

Robert was surprised at Marge's order. "Same here," he said with a slight smile.

They sat there, sipping their bourbon, when a young man came over and sat beside them. He seemed quite familiar with Marge, Robert noticed.

"So this is your new friend," the man said, looking at Robert suspiciously.

Marge laughed. "No, Mike. I just met him today. He is new around here."

"Hi, Robert." Mike offered a hand. "Welcome to the neighborhood."

His grip was weak. And the way he dressed told Robert that he was not in competition for Marge's friendship.

"So you are working with that Pete. Don't let him work your ass off," Mike told him.

"He nearly did it today, but I'll catch on tomorrow," Robert said with confidence.

Mike was not so sure. Downing his drink, he muttered, "Good luck with that." He stumbled on his way out the door.

Marge looked at Robert with an inquisitive look, trying to learn more about him. "Where do you live?" she asked.

"About two blocks from here, on Bay Street," he told her.

"Thanks for the drinks." With that, she stood up and walked out the door, leaving him alone at the bar.

Exhausted and alone, Robert decided to go home. When he walked into his place and saw how empty it was, he had not realized how alone he would be without his buddies. The only food he had was a dozen eggs, a can of mackerel, and a half gallon of orange juice that Bob had left.

He prepared some fish and eggs for supper. Then went out on the second floor porch and enjoyed a beautiful view. He sat there until it started getting late or maybe it was the bugs that ran him off the porch. He was thinking that Marge was a beautiful girl and that maybe he should ask her out. On second thought, he said to himself. "Maybe I'd better wait until I've worked for a few weeks."

The next morning, he was up and at it early. His intention was to show Pete and the captain that he could hold his own with any man. When he got to the dock that morning, the captain and Pete was already on the boat waiting for him. Captain Lowe gave him a wave. "Welcome aboard," the captain said, while engaging the gear of the boat. They headed southwest to the fishing area.

As the boat set sail, Pete nodded to Robert. "How are you doing?" he asked. Then he turned to the captain and yelled, "We are going to get a bunch of shrimp today, ain't we, Captain?"

"Yeah, I hope so," Captain Lowe replied, looking up at the sky. "It sure is a beautiful day to try."

First, the captain headed toward an area where he was sure to get a lot of action. He had noticed that there were no boats there, but he decided to put his nets down anyway.

After he let out his nets and searched for an hour or so, when he pulled the nets in, there were hardly a bushel of shrimp. "I was sure that there would be some shrimp here this morning," the captain mumbled. He took out his binoculars and looked around the area. He could not see any sign of boats. "Pull in the nets," he said. "We have got to go hunting."

"Let's go hunting!" Pete yelled. He jumped to his feet and grabbed the net. Immediately, Robert followed Pete's action. To the captain's delight, the nets were on board in short order.

"Grab the glasses, Pete," the captain said as he walked the deck of the boat. "See what you can find."

While the captain readied his vessel, Pete searched for any sign of boats. Robert was doing the best he could to get the nets in as good condition as he could in anticipation of what they might find.

They had been searching for about twenty-five minutes when Pete yelled out, "Birds on the port side thirty degrees south by southeast."

The captain immediately reacted to the sound of Pete's voice. "There are boats headed that way!" Pete yelled. "They must be on to something."

"I see them," Captain Lowe yelled. "There must be some shrimp out there."

Excited, Pete went over and made a few adjustments to the nets and readied himself to release the nets as soon as the captain gave the word. At first, it was hard to tell but they were closer to the birds than the other boats.

"Get ready to let the net out!" Captain Lowe cried out.

Pete and Robert both rushed to their respected position. Pete smiled when he saw that Robert was in his position and ready to go. When the call to let out the nets came, both men went to work, like a well-oiled machine. It was a good day. They had filled their nets with lots of shrimp and now they were heading back to the dock. The captain felt good about his new man, seeing how well he worked under pressure.

It was one of those perfect days to be out on the water. The surface was as flat as a sheet. The gulls were flying low over the wake of the boat and the clouds hung low; they were beautifully white and fluffy. In this peacefulness, Robert was quiet. He had serious thoughts of going back to school and he also wanted to earn enough money to stick around long enough to get to know Marge.

The day had gone very well. Robert had tried his best to keep up with Pete. He had done his best so that the captain would keep him around for a few more days. The captain was pleased with his work and complimented him on doing such a good job.

After work, Robert went for a walk down to the bar expecting to see Marge, but she was not there. So sitting at the bar, having a drink alone, made him feel a bit out of place. Without her there, no one bothered to come over to speak to him so he decided to go home, buy himself some groceries, cook a meal, and then get a good night's sleep.

He went out on the second floor porch to take a break before going down to the store. While sitting there on his porch, he saw a woman walking toward his flat. As the person drew nearer, he could see that it was Marge. He could already recognize the rhythm of her steps and the curves of her body.

"So this is where you live," she said with a quick chuckle as she approached his apartment.

Robert was very happy to see her. "Come on up," he replied.

She strolled into his place and sat down at the table.

"Look," she said, holding up a brown bottle. "I brought you some rum. Do you like rum?"

"Yes," Robert replied.

Sitting at his table, he was seeing her for the first time. Her silky ebony hair flowed down on both sides of her shoulders like silk curtains around a window that overlooks a field of flowers. He could not help but stare for a moment. Then he heard her say.

"Do you know how to fish?" Marge said as she looked around his place, her eyes missing nothing.

Robert played the game. "I do okay, but I don't have any fishing gear," he told her.

"Don't worry about it, I have plenty. Meet me at my stand tomorrow and I'll have gear for the both of us. We can go out on the pier and see if we can catch some fish."

Robert had some shrimp that he had brought home for food, but he had been too lazy to cook them, so he decided to use them for bait. Marge got up from the outside table and went into Robert's kitchen. She found two glasses in the sink. As she poured the liquor, she asked him if he liked living in New Orleans.

"It's okay. There were three of us when we first moved in here."

"What happened to the other two guys?"

"They went back to college."

"Where were they going to school?"

"In Baton Rouge."

"Are you planning to go back to school?"

"I'm planning to go back next semester." He finally realized that he was being checked out. Marge was getting to know everything about him.

Marge gave him a sly look. "That sound like a good idea, I think." Then she got up from her chair, finished her drink, and left without a word.

The next morning, they met at the fishing stand. She was wearing blue short shorts with a red shirt. The bottom of the shirt was tied with a knot covering her belly button. On her head, she wore a white Panama hat. On her feet were white shoes to match the hat. She was carrying two fishing rods and a small tackle box.

Robert was wearing blue jeans and a polo shirt, and he was carrying a bucket with the extra shrimp bait. Marge had some soft shell crabs and a dozen blood worms to add to the bait bucket. They walked down to the jetty that projected out into the gulf for about one fourth of a mile. The day was nice and cool with a calm wind. The sun was a big red glow that was just beginning to show itself.

They sat there on the jetty at the edge of the gulf. Handing Robert a rod, Marge motioned to the tackle box. "The hooks are in there," she said.

Robert sat the bait bucket between the two of them. He baited his hook and casted his line out about twenty yards, then offered to help her bait her hook.

Marge scowled, "I have been fishing all my life, remember?"

She baited her hook, threw it about ten feet from the edge of the jetty, and let it sink to the bottom. Within three minutes, there was a jerk on the line. "Got you," she whispered while reeling in a croaker.

"Is that what you come out here for?" Robert asked, he was amused.

"I'm just getting ready to fish." Marge laughed. "This croaker is my bait."

Marge fished for a few more croakers, cut them into small pieces to be used for bait. Then she started casting out into deeper water, letting the bait settle down to the bottom. She started jigging the bait. A few minutes later, she felt a strong tug on her line. Her rod bent over and started vibrating excitedly.

"I got you," Marge yelled with conviction. "That's what I'm talking about!" she screamed excitedly. "That's what I came out here for." She laughed as she reeled the fish in.

Robert had been watching her every move. He jumped up seeing how excited she was. "You got him! Pull him in." He was ecstatic. She pulled in a twenty-pound red drum. The next time she baited her hook, Robert paid close attention to what she was doing, for he had never seen such a big, beautiful fish. Now he was out to get one for himself. He casted as close to her fishing area as possible. He caught a couple of croakers but no red drums. She could see that he was doing the best that he could, but he had no luck. She felt bad for him; however, she offered no help.

Marge caught and released three other large red drums before she asked him if he was ready to go.

"Yes," Robert said as the two of them began to gather their fish and equipment. This time, they went to her place.

Her place was similar to his, but the neatness and decor overwhelmed him. It was so clean and neat that it made him feel a bit of shame.

"You can clean up in there," Marge said, pointing to the bathroom, "while I clean the fish." She put her tackle box and rods away, cleaned herself up, and came back to the kitchen to do the cooking. Meanwhile, Robert cleaned himself up, poured himself a drink, and sat down to relax.

Marge was frying the freshly caught drum. The aroma reminded him of Sarah's cooking. The fish covered with butter, lemon juice, onion, and the well-known trinity seasoning of New Orleans. She served sliced tomatoes over lettuce, sprinkled with a bit of salt and vinegar. Her corn bread was made with green and red hot peppers, chopped onions, and a dash of hot sauce. It was wonderful. They spent the rest of the day out on the front porch together, enjoying the food and relaxing in the warm Gulf Coast sun.

Sitting there with his feet resting on the rail, Robert asked if she lived there alone. She told him that she did and that she felt comfortable being alone. She could come and go as she pleased with no one to answer to. "Besides I have my work friends and my parents close by. That's enough to keep me busy and out of trouble," Marge said, then she looked over to his side of the porch and asked, "What do you do when you quit work?"

Robert watched Marge closely. "I don't know yet," he said. "When my friends were here, we would go out for beers but now that they've gone, I guess I'll have to find something else to do."

"If you don't mind, we can get together every now and then," she said. It was a nice day so Marge walked Robert half way back to his place all the while chatting and talking about the good times that they had had that day.

A few days passed after their dinner and Robert could not keep his mind off her. His ability to concentrate on his job was such that the captain had to call him in and speak to him again about his work. All of his thoughts were on her and how he was going back to school and keep in contact with her at the same time. His first priority was to get back into school, but he needed transportation to keep seeing her. He also needed this job so he had to concentrate on his work as well.

That evening, he stopped by Marge's stand wanting to speak with her. She didn't seem surprised.

"What's up?" she asked.

"I'm going back to school…and I would like to know if I could continue to see you," Robert said nervously.

Marge looked at him and asked, "How are you going to do that?" Knowing that if he went back to school, he might find another girl and start seeing her.

"I'll ask my parents if they will get me a car. That way, I can drive down here from school."

"Do your parents have that kind of money?"

Still nervous, Robert replied, "I think that I can talk them into it."

Marge remained uncommitted. "When you get your car, come on down here to see me, then we'll talk." With that, she went back to her stand.

The following Friday, Robert went back to college.

After a week or so, Mrs. Williams received a letter from Robert. She sat in a chair in the living room next to Mr. Williams reading it. Her husband really wasn't paying that much attention until she came to the part about his son asking for a car. Hearing his wife read about his son asking about buying a car disappointed him.

"What was that about a car?" Mr. Williams looked up from his paper and asked.

"Robert says that he's back in school now and he wants you to buy him a car." Mrs. Williams knew that a request from Robert would upset his father, so she wanted to wait and talk to him later when he was more relaxed.

"I thought he had a job," Mr. Williams replied with a bit of irritation.

His wife saw he was getting aggravated, so she said quietly, "We need to keep him in school so that when he comes home, he'll know how to run the farm."

Mr. Williams folded his paper. He was reluctant but he knew his wife was right. "Okay, okay," he said. "We'll get him a car but he had better get himself together." Mr. Williams stood up saying, as he walked into the kitchen, "I'm getting tired of him wasting money."

With his father's money, Robert bought a red, two-door Ford with a rumble seat, just like his friend Tommy's car. With his ride, he could go see Marge and go to school as well.

CHAPTER 3

IT HAD BEEN seven months since Sarah and Bert had slept together. It was obvious that she was having a baby, yet they had not spoken of it with each other. Fanny would come by on a regular basis, hoping to be around in case Sarah went into labor. According to Bert's calculation, Sarah had about two more months to go before giving birth.

It was about two weeks later, Sarah was at the Williams's house cooking supper when the pains hit her. "Oh my god! It's my time... I'm going to have this baby," she screamed. The next pain was harder than the first.

Mrs. Williams was calm. "Come with me," she told Sarah. "I'm going to take you home. We'll stop by and pick up Fanny so she can help you." Fanny, the midwife of the neighborhood, was always ready for such an emergency, and because she knew that Sarah was pregnant, she was prepared for the occasion.

Quickly, Mrs. Williams turned off the kerosene stove, removed the pots from the fire, and walked Sarah to her car. She drove with Sarah in the front seat breathing through the pain to Fanny's place. The midwife got into the car and they all headed to Sarah's house.

As Bert approached the house, he heard his wife scream and somehow he knew that the baby had arrived. He rushed in and there on the bed was his wife screaming in pain. Bert couldn't help but think about the last time they had been together and believed that she was about to have an early birth. But in the back of his mind, he thought, things don't always happen the way you think they should.

It was about three o'clock that next morning. Fanny, the midwife of Swamp Town, was going along performing a skillful job, doing her midwife duties while Bert stood by waiting for his first baby born. He stood there, patiently and quiet, waiting to see his first baby born into this world.

When it happened, the baby came out having all the Caucasian features, including the blue eyes, skin color, and blond hair. Bert just stood there, eyes wide open, and a single tear fell down from his eyes. Fanny watched as Bert's legs buckled. She felt his pain and surprise. She could see that he had finally learned why Sarah was so withdrawn.

Bert just stood there, his legs trembling; a tear ran down his cheeks. His heart beat faster and faster, driving more and more blood to his brain, trying to control the rage that was growing there. He slowly turned and moved without direction or purpose and walked out of the house.

Bert went to the pasture and sat on the rail, trying to find some place to control his rage. He saw the fog forming in the fields and watched as the soft orange glow of the sun rays gave notice that a new day was dawning. This was a day that Bert would not welcome. He climbed down off the rail. Slowly, he walked to the barn, then to the creek, carrying a rope in his hands. He got into his dingy and rowed out to an old cypress tree stump that had a decaying limb that protruded about six feet beyond the base of the stump. He stood up, threw the rope over the limb, placed the rope around his neck, and kicked the dingy from under his feet. He hung there; his feet barely touching the surface of the water.

Fanny did what she could for Sarah. It was midday before she got a break. She walked to the door to see if she could see Bert, then she looked out at the rail of the pasture where he always sat when he wanted to relax or needed time to get himself together. Bert was nowhere to be seen. She walked back into the house with a worried look in her eyes and she wondered if he had left her. When Fanny walked back into Sarah's bedroom, she could see the worried look in Sarah's face.

"Don't worry," Fanny told her. "He'll be home soon."

Fanny cleaned the baby off and wrapped it in clean clothes and then she laid the baby in Sarah's arms. "I'm going to Mrs. Jones's house and ask her if she will come over here and relieve me for a while so I can take a break...Don't worry," she said as she gave her friend a soft hug. "He'll be back soon."

Fanny saw Ray Jr. as she approached the Jones house. "Ray Jr.! Ray Jr.!" she called, her voice was full of concern. Fanny was so tired and in need of rest.

Ray Jr. walked out onto the front porch.

"Yes, Miss Fanny?" he answered.

"Ask your mother to come here," she said.

"Mom!" Ray Jr. yelled. "Miss Fanny wants to see you."

Mrs. Jones came outside and walked over to where Fanny stood. She could see that what Fanny had to say was not for the boy's ears.

"Sarah had the baby," Fanny whispered.

"How's she doing?" Mrs. Jones asked.

"Okay," she said as she turned around making sure that they were alone. "But Bert is not there."

"Where is he?" Mrs. Jones asked. "Where could he be at a time like this?"

"I don't know," Fanny replied. Then she asked, "Will you go over there and be with her for a while so I can take a break? I'll be back soon to let you get back to what you were doing."

With Ray Jr. and Ben's mother gone, the two boys decided to take a trip down to the creek and try to catch a few catfish. They walked to the place where Bert kept his dingy, but it was not there. They looked over toward the place where Bert usually caught the large catfish, thinking that Bert might be there trying to get a nice one for supper. Then Ray Jr. heard a bloodcurdling scream. Ray Jr. turned to look for his brother who screamed again. When he heard Ben this time, he ran toward his brother who was standing there shaking and crying. "It's him. It's him!" Ben cried out with tears running down his cheeks and fear in his eyes.

"It's Mr. Bert. They killed him. They killed Mr. Bert," Ben cried.

Bert was hanging there. His feet was three inches into the water. His boat had drifted over to an adjacent cypress tree. The paddles resting where he had left them. The two boys ran as fast as they could and met their father who was now just leaving home for a hard day's work in the field. As the boys got closer to their father, he heard the younger boy sobbing. "They killed him, they killed him," the boy cried.

"Who killed who?" Ray said as he tried to calm his sons down.

"We don't know," Ray Jr. cried. "He's been hung down at the creek."

The three of them met one of the tenants, James Whitfield, who lived in one of the houses at the other end of Swamp Town. He had seen the boys running to meet their father. James, who had no idea what was going on, saw that there may be a problem, so he rushed over and offered to give them a hand. The four of them rushed back down to the creek and found Bert where the boys had said he would be. Ray and James jumped into the water and waded out to the boat. They climbed into the dingy and rowed it over to the cypress tree. Without a word, they lowered Bert's body down into the boat and took him to the bank of the creek. Meanwhile, Ray Jr. had gone to the barn to get a mule and cart to place Bert's body in.

They took Bert's body home but held him outside until Ray could speak to Sarah. He did not know that his wife was there so when he saw her, he pulled her aside and whispered the bad news to his wife. When Sarah heard the news, she was overwhelmed by grief and cried out," I'm so sorry, Bert!" I should have told you.

The birth of Sarah's son and the death of Bert caused a cloud of gloom to hang over Swamp Town for weeks. Jessie Mae, who was Bert's first love, suffered most of all. They had broken up years earlier, but she had stuck around Swamp Town so that she could see him and be his friend even if she couldn't be his lover. Her heart held the tears for a lost lover. but she had to shed them in secret. Many late evenings, she'd walk the path down by the creek and cry over her lost love.

Sarah now had a newborn baby and no man to tend the crops that Bert had taken care of, so Mr. Williams had to get someone else to tend the farm. Sarah continued to work for Mrs. Williams, but with the baby, she was not able to take care of the work that Bert had been doing. Mrs. Williams had her moved to an empty house on the path leading to the big house. The house had three rooms with plenty of open area around it.

The house that Sarah moved into was smaller but much closer to her work, and she was told by Mrs. Williams that she could bring the baby to work with her.

The family who moved into Sarah's old home was Sam Wilson, his wife Mavis, their two sons, and their baby girl Alice. The Wilsons had come to Swamp Town from the north side of Baton Rouge. Sam was a well-built, light-skinned man, about five feet eight inches tall. His wife was a dark-skinned, heavyset woman, who was about two inches taller than her husband was. The two boys were age three and five years old, while baby Alice was in her first year.

A few days after the baby was born, Fanny came by to see her. She held the baby in her arms. "What do you call him?" Fanny asked.

"Baby," Sarah said. She looked at her son sadly and not even considered naming the baby boy.

"You just can't call a person baby," Fanny said.

"Yeah I know," Sarah said. "What would you call him?"

Fanny bounced the boy in her lap. "What about Bert?" she asked.

"No," Sarah said slowly. "No, I can't do that. Not to my Bert." Not wanting that name to remind her of the sadness that she had caused Bert.

"I had an uncle named Josh. What about Josh?" Fanny suggested.

"That sounds nice." Sarah gave Fanny a slight smile. "Yeah, that sounds nice. I'll call him Josh."

Robert Jr. had returned to school. He had his car and was traveling to New Orleans regularly to see Marge. He was now living in her place on his visits to the Gulf. Marge wanted to go to Swamp Town to see his parents' place, but he had never invited her and she had not gotten up the nerve to ask him to take her there. It had been a month since she had seen him and Robert was coming to see her that weekend. She had a very important surprise to tell him and could hardly wait until he came through the door.

Most times when Robert Jr. visited her, he would bring one or two of his friends with him, but today he was riding alone and didn't have to leave them at a hotel. He could pick her up at her fish stand if he gets there in time.

He had a busy time schedule. He was packing all of his belongings into his car and would then have to go by registration to check out. He would pick up his grades and finally head for the Gulf. It was the end of Robert's last class and he was anticipating his final grades. He hoped they would be good enough for him to graduate with a degree in business and that would please his parents.

He had not anticipated such a long wait but the grades did not come out until five o'clock, so he waited on campus until the grades were posted. When he got his paperwork, he was a nervous wreck and could not see himself spending another semester in that school, so when he looked at his grades he was filled with joy. He had passed all of his classes. He could now go to New Orleans, pick up Marge and take her to her place and spend the night. If she agreed, he would take her tomorrow to his parents' house to meet them.

By the time Robert got to the Gulf, Marge had left her fishing stand for the night. Robert arrived at Marge's place at about nine o'clock that night. When he entered the house, Marge was filled with excitement. She could not wait to tell him the good news.

"I'm pregnant!" she shouted with excitement as soon as he walked into the house. Marge was ecstatic and Robert was shocked. He was thinking how could he take a pregnant girl home to see his mother whose Catholic upbringing would not allow her to even think of sex before marriage.

"Say something, honey. Aren't you happy we're having a baby?" Marge had not noticed Robert's apprehension. She was waiting for a chance to fall into his arms.

"Yeah, honey. I'm happy," Robert replied. "I just wanted to get married first."

"We can get married when we get to your home, can't we?" she asked the question and had not considered that there might be a problem.

Marge was already talking, *we*, and speaking of his parents place as home.

"We'll see," Robert said. Things were moving a bit too fast for him. He had to think fast but his love overruled his reasoning. He had to go home and show his parents that he had really completed college and his love for Marge dictated that he take her with him. His mind raced around in his head, trying to think of something to tell his parents but nothing was there, so he thought, *I'll think of something tomorrow.*

CHAPTER 4

THEY ARRIVED IN Swamp Town the following morning. The Williamses expected him but Marge was a surprise. They entered the property from the main road and drove up the horseshoe drive way to the front of the house. Mrs. Williams met him on the porch. He rushed over to his mother, gave her a big hug, all the while saying, "Hello, Mom, How are you? How have you been?

"How have you been, son?" Mrs. Williams said as she hugged him. Then she turned and looked at Marge. "And who is that lovely girl?" she asked.

"That's my girlfriend, Mom. I wrote you about her," Robert said, grinning as he spoke.

"Yeah, but you didn't tell me that she was so pretty."

Marge was now out of the car, walking up the steps. "Hello," she said as Mr. Williams walked through the front door.

"Hello! Hello!" Mr. Williams said as he walked over and hugged them both.

"Come on in the house." Mrs. Williams invited the two of them into their home. They all sat down in the parlor. Sarah came out of the kitchen, carrying a tray with coffee. She served the four of them and walked back into the kitchen without saying a word.

"And who is this young lady?" Mrs. Williams asked again.

Without thinking or hesitation, Robert Jr. declared, "This is the girl that I'm going to marry."

Mrs. Williams was in shock, while her husband was filled with joy and congratulated him.

"When is the date?" his father asked.

"This weekend," Marge said. "If it's all right with you two."

Mr. Williams turned to his wife. "Is that all right with you, honey?" he asked.

Robert was shocked at how fast everything was happening, but he didn't want to tell his mother about the baby, so he ran with it. "It's okay by me if it's all right with you, Mom."

"It's okay with me," Mrs. Williams said looking at Marge with renewed interest.

She then looked at them both. "You two are going to have to sleep in separate rooms until then," she said.

Robert stood up and took Marge around and showed her the place. Marge was amazed at how large the place was.

After the young couple left the room, Mrs. Williams looked at her husband with concern. "Don't you think that they were moving too fast?" she asked her husband.

"Moving too fast?" he said. "They have been shacking up for months. It's time for him to settle down and start to work. Starting tomorrow, I'm going to start showing him how to run this place. I'll take him around so he can meet the tenants."

"I guess you are right," she said. "Maybe he'll give us a grandson."

The next morning, Mr. Williams took his son for a tour of the plantation. His purpose was to show him how the place was to be supervised.

"Robert," he said, referring to the black workers. These people are not slaves anymore." You've got to remember that and treat them accordingly.

"I know," Robert said.

With deep concern, he spoke to his son, saying, "A lot of people around here think that they have lost a way of life, but I personally think that, in the long run, everyone will be better off. It's only been forty years or so since the war has ended and already we have black teachers, inventors, and have you heard about that guy Carver at Tuskegee? I wouldn't be a bit surprised how well they will be doing in the next fifty years."

"Why do you say that, Dad?" Robert said with a puzzled look on his face. "Won't we have to take care of them?"

Mr. Williams explained, "We don't own them anymore, we own the land. They take care of the land and the land takes care of all of us. You've got to learn that they are free now. They can come and go as they please." He looked at his son, trying to make sure that he understood what his father was trying to tell him. I believe if we treat them fairly and let them tend the land, we'll all be happier."

"I did learn something after I left home, Dad," Robert said. "I went to work on a shrimp boat in New Orleans and had to work side by side with a black man. At first, I thought that I was the one to tell him how to do the work. The captain told me that I had to work with him. At first, I had a problem but later I got used to working with him."

"After you've worked with these people a while, you'll get used to working with them and after a while you will realize that we all have a lot in common," Mr. Williams replied.

Mr. Williams looked at his son, this time, with pride. "I know what you mean, son." Then he added, "If you are not careful, you might even find a friend."

"I understand what you are saying, Dad."

"What do you mean, Junior?"

Robert spoke, saying, "This guy, Pete, who worked on the boat with the captain. One afternoon when we got off work, he asked me if I would have a beer with him. I agreed and we went to a bar on a street in his neighborhood. I don't know why but I was surprised to find that music was playing, guys were sitting around drinking beer and having fun just as they did in any other bar. All of Pete's friends spoke to me and asked me what my name was. Pete told them and we all sat at the bar. No one seemed to care whether I was there or not. When we left, they just said come again any time."

Robert's father was gazing straight ahead. He did not say a word, but he knew that his son had learned a good lesson. They rode over the entire plantation. Mr. Williams showed his son some of the property that his son had never seen. On the way back to the house, Junior turned to his father and asked, "Why are you showing me all of this?"

"One day," Mr. Williams said. "You're going to have to run this place and it can't be run like a slave plantation anymore."

Mrs. Williams gave Marge a tour of the plantation home. "Do you think that you could live here?" She asked as she watched Marge intently, trying to pick up clues on what she was thinking. "This is a large place, are you suggesting that we stay here after we are married?" Marge asked.

"Why not?" Mrs. Williams said. "Don't you like this place?"

"Of course, I do." Marge replied. "This place is beautiful. I love it." In her mind, she was saying, *Would you want me to if you knew that I was pregnant?*

They walked through the upstairs, all the bedrooms, and the parlor. As they entered the kitchen, Mrs. Williams smiled and said, "This is Sarah's domain. She works for me. She cooks and cleans, and I have given her the right to bring her two-year-old boy with her when she needs to. Do you see any problems with that?"

"Not at all," Marge said.

Mrs. Williams asked Sarah to serve the two of them coffee, then they went back into the parlor and relaxed while enjoying their coffee.

Mr. Williams and his son entered the parlor, still talking about the property and how it should be managed. Mr. Williams went to the kitchen door and asked Sarah to bring two more coffees.

"How do you like yours?" he asked his son.

"Black with one spoon of sugar," he said.

"Have you suggested to Marge that they live here after they are married?" Mr. Williams asked his wife.

His wife gave him a wink. "Yes," Mrs. Williams said. "I gave her a hint."

"Well," Mr. Williams said, "if no one has any objections, the two of you can have the upstairs area. What do you say?"

Robert agreed.

"I'll be happy where ever you are, honey," Marge added.

It was a couple of months after the young couple had moved in that Mrs. Williams found out why Mr. Williams wanted his son to move in with them and learn how to manage the plantation.

Mr. Williams had gone to work in Baton Rouge. Sarah had cleaned their bedroom and found a piece of paper on the floor that she thought was important. She placed it on the nightstand and when Mrs. Williams found the paper, she learned that her husband had colon cancer. She was devastated and had to get to the doctor in Baton Rouge to find out what was going on. The doctor confirmed what the report had said and she now knew why he wanted their son to be able to take over the management of the plantation but wondered why he hadn't told her.

The doctor told Mr. Williams that his wife had found out that he was seriously ill. Mr. Williams was concerned and wondered how she had found out so when he arrived back home, he drove up to the front door, blew his horn, and motioned for his wife to come to the car. The two of them rode around the plantation and spoke of the inevitable for hours.

Mrs. Williams was upset with him but she couldn't get angry with him. "Why didn't you tell me this was going on?" she asked.

"I didn't want you to worry," he said. "There is no need for you to worry for months and months. I was going to tell you when the time got close."

"I'm your wife," she said. "I need to know what's going on with you." She was not angry, just hurt that he had kept something this important from her. "From now on," she told him, "I'm going to the doctor with you."

"I'm sorry that you had to find out this way, honey," he told her. On their way back to the house, they were both silent.

When they arrived at the house, they sat there for a moment. "My problem was the reason I wanted them to get married and move into the house. I wanted someone to be with you when I got so I couldn't help myself," Mr. Williams said quietly.

"Did you know that Marge was with child?" his wife asked.

"No," Mr. Williams said. "How did you know?"

"She told me a week ago."

"I guess we all keep secrets sometimes."

"Are you going to tell Junior about your problem now?"

"No," he said. "We'll tell him when the pain gets worse. The doctor said that it won't be long."

They went into the kitchen and sat at the table. Mr. Williams seemed at ease. He asked Sarah to get them coffee and inquired about her son. "How old is Josh now?" Mr. Williams asked.

Sarah gave him his coffee and wondered why he cared. "He was a year old last month." She left to continue her daily duties.

While the young Williams was out checking the crops. Marge noticed that the house that Sarah used to live in had all of the livestock, and the tenant living there took care of them. Being curious, she asked Junior, "Why one man had to take care of all of the livestock?"

"That's the way it's always been," Junior replied.

Marge thought for a moment. "What if they raise their own livestock and shared that, the same as they shared all of the other crops. I think that would be better for everyone."

"I'll look into that and see how it works."

When they got home, the young couple went into the house and could see that their parents were in the kitchen.

"Join us," Mr. Williams said. "Pour yourself a cup of coffee." He watched the young couple as they made themselves comfortable. "What have you two been up to?" he asked.

"Just checking the area, seeing how the crops are coming along," Marge said.

Junior nodded. "Marge suggested that maybe we should split up the livestock and let each tenant take care of his own and share them the same as they shares the other crops."

His parents were intrigued. "I think that's a good idea," his mom said.

His dad agreed. "Looks like that's going to be one of your first official projects," Mr. Williams told him.

Junior noticed a change in his father's voice. There was apprehension. "What do you mean?" Junior asked slowly. He saw a quick glance between the two of them. Mrs. Williams could see in her husband's eyes that now was the time to tell Junior what was going on with his father.

"I'm going to turn over the operation of the plantation to you," his father said.

Junior sensed some sadness. "Why?" his son asked.

Seeing the distress in her husband's eyes, Mrs. Williams gave her son the bad news.

Marge and Junior had been married for six months now and her pregnancy had been showing for some time. Marge had been up before Sarah had come in to prepare breakfast. Sarah offered to get Marge some coffee as she entered the kitchen and saw that Marge was looking a bit pale.

"No," said Marge. "I'm just feeling a little under the weather this morning."

Sarah knew how she felt. She had been under the weather many times, especially when she was pregnant with Josh. She figured Marge was close to giving birth. "When are you due?" Sarah asked.

"Pretty soon," said Marge, who sat down with a groan. Sarah knew what Marge meant and shook her head in agreement because she could see that Marge had a bit of a smile on her face.

"Let's just call it an early birth," Marge replied. Marge and Junior's baby, Brenda, was born two weeks later.

CHAPTER 5

THE COUNTY DECIDED to build an elementary school for black children about two miles from Swamp Town. Josh was now six years old and Sarah wanted to enroll him into the new school. At first, she had feared the idea of insisting that her son attended the school. She had anticipated an objection from the Williamses, knowing that in the past they had insisted the children of the tenants stay on the farm and work. This bothered her until she had a talk with Jesse Mae.

It had been a long time since Sarah had spoken with Jesse Mae. She had gone for a walk with Josh and decided to stop by Jesse Mae's place. It was around two thirty on a Saturday and Jesse's son, Mark, was in the bar cleaning up when Sarah and Josh walked in.

"Hi, Mark," Sarah said as she settled into a chair. "Is Jesse here?"

Mark finished wiping a table. "Yes, ma'am. She's in the back. I'll call her." Mark called his mom. "Mom, Miss Sarah's here to see you."

"I'll be right there," Miss Mae yelled.

As Jesse entered the bar, she was surprised to see Sarah and her son there. They exchanged pleasantries. Jesse joined Sarah at her table. She had her son bring them cold drinks and wondered why Sarah needed to visit.

"It's kind of hot out there today. What were you doing out there in all that sun?" said Sarah.

"Oh, just cleaning off my grill, getting ready for tonight," Jesse said. "What brings you by here?"

Sarah fiddled with her glass. "I needed someone to talk to. You know that they have built a new school and I have been thinking about taking Josh there."

With a nod, Jesse said, "Don't think about it, just do it."

"I was worried about what the Williams would say. What if they don't want him to go to that school? I'd have to keep him out of school or move."

Jesse looked at Sarah. "So be it. There are other ways to make a living. They have nothing to do with your child going to school. He needs an education and it's your place to see that he gets it."

"Thank you," Sarah said. She was at ease now. "May I ask you a question?" She continued to fiddle with her glass. After hesitating for a few seconds, she said, "Why have you always been so nice to me?"

Jesse Mae was surprised that she asked the question but understood why she asked it. "As you know," she said, "Bert and I was a couple in the early days. I suppose you and everyone else knew that we had broken up before you met him. I want you to know that it was me who broke up with him. It was all my fault." Jesse sighed. "I treated him wrong. I went up north, trying to find a job and a better way of life but all I found was bitter cold and misery." Sarah could see the tears in her eyes when she said. "And all I came home with was a bun in the oven."

"I didn't mean to upset you," Sarah told Jesse.

"That's okay. I had a chance to get back with him but we had a fight and I told him that I never wanted to see him again. He begged me, but I wouldn't go back to him. Then he met you. I was hurt. I was very hurt, but I could see that he was in love with you. I knew that if I interfered with his relationship with you, I would still lose him. I was just glad that he remained my friend. When I found out that he had died, late in the evenings, I would go down to the creek where he used to fish. I'd sit there by his boat and cry until late in the night."

Sarah was surprised. "Why did you go down there?" she asked.

"I wanted to be alone and I didn't want anyone to know that I was crying over your man," said Jesse.

"I want to thank you for not going after Bert, Jesse." Sarah was sincere. She could see how much Jesse loved her husband.

"Oh, that would not have worked." Jesse said. "Bert was a one-woman man. When he was with me, he was only with me. When he was with you, I knew he was with you. There was no point in creating a problem for all three of us, and I knew that he would not leave you for me."

"Thanks for telling me this," Sarah said. "I'm glad that you are a friend."

Two days after her conversation with Jesse Mae, that Saturday morning, Sarah woke up in a sad mood. She was thinking of Bert and couldn't get it off her mind. She had not slept well lately and had no desire to eat, so Sarah sat on her front porch, thinking of how horrible it was and how painful it must have been for Bert. He was expecting his first son and there lying on his bed was his wife who had just given birth to a white child. He had worked hard all of his life, served his country, worked for practically nothing. And now he had nothing, not even the will to live. Bert was a good man, but it seemed that life had been exceptionally cruel to him.

Sarah had just finished her house work but had no need to prepare food for herself. From her house, she could see Mrs.

Williams in her garden working with her flowers. Sarah got up from her chair with no particular reason on her mind and started walking in the direction of the flower garden. There was no need to hurry. It was a pleasant day and there was plenty of daylight left.

Sarah entered the garden and walked toward Mrs. Williams, admiring the flowers as she went. She walked along, lightly touching a blossom here and there. When she got close, she said, "Hello, Mrs. Williams, I see you're enjoying your flowers."

"Yeah," Mrs. Williams said. "I don't believe I've ever seen you out here."

"No," Sarah replied. "I was just sitting out there on the porch, thinking of what I did to Bert. How I kept the secret from him. My Lord, it must have made him feel so bad." Her voice was trembling as she continued, trying to make some sense out of what had happen to her life, and Mrs. Williams was the only one around with a shoulder that she could cry on.

"What you did to Bert," Mrs. Williams said to Sarah, "it was I who talked you into keeping your mouth shut. I wanted to protect my family. I didn't know what to do. I didn't know what I was doing to you." A tear ran down her cheek and fell to the ground.

Sarah went to her side and wiped the tears from her face, then Sarah started sobbing. All at once, the pains had overwhelmed her. Then Sarah sat in a chair that Mrs. Williams used for taking a break while she worked in the garden. Mrs. Williams walked over to Sarah and put her arms around her shoulder. They cried in each other's arms and found a bit of piece that the two of them could share.

"I feel so bad," Sarah said. "I should have told him! I should have told him!" She cried. "I do not believe that he would have killed himself if I had just told him!"

Mrs. Williams started toward the house, then she stopped, turned and said, "Sarah, come to the house with me."

Sarah followed her to the house, and when they got to the house, they had a seat in the parlor. Mrs. Williams went to the kitchen. When she returned, she had coffee for the two of them. After they had finish their coffee, Mrs. Williams asked Sarah to pray with her. She prayed while Sarah held her hands. The prayer and friendship created a bond between the two of them.

"Thanks for asking me to pray with you," Sarah said to Mrs. Williams. "I feel better now and I'll see you tomorrow." On her way back to her porch, she felt better about sharing her pain and prayers with Mrs. Williams.

For the first time, Swamp Town had a school for black children and it was now open. Sarah had dressed Josh in bib overalls, a white tee shirt and high top shoes. Her plan was to walk Josh to school but Josh was running five to ten yards ahead of her. He could not wait to get into this new building—this place of learning. When they got to the school, there were only six students there. The teacher, Mr. Smith, was a young man, about thirty years of age, a small man with light skin, a bit timid but a man who loved children.

Mr. Smith sat at his desk. There were only two benches for the students to sit on and a blackboard behind the teacher's desk.

Mr. Smith got up from his seat to greet Sarah and her son. After he introduced himself, Sarah wanted him to meet her son Josh.

"This is Josh. He wants to come to this school," she said.

"Welcome." Mr. Smith smiled. "Come in and have a seat," he said to Josh.

A taller bench was located in front of the smaller bench and was used for a desk. On those benches were placed a pad and a pencil for each student. The shorter bench was placed behind the taller one and used as seats. The four girls sat in the front row while the two boys sat in the second row. Josh was now officially a student.

Sarah rushed back to the Williams's place to get back to work. When she walked in, Mrs. Williams was just getting up for the day. Because Sarah had already prepared the food, all she had to do was plate it and serve.

When Mrs. Williams came into the kitchen, Sarah tried to make small talk. "How was your night's sleep?" Sarah was nervous as she watched the woman lift her fork.

"Fine," Mrs. Williams said. "Did you get Josh registered in school this morning?"

Sarah was shocked. She had no idea that Mrs. Williams knew about the school or that Josh was old enough to attend.

"Yes," said Sarah, who was now proud and happy that she had brought up the subject. "My boy is now in school."

Mrs. Williams was happy as well. "Good," she said. "I'm glad you have him in school. I want to see him grow up and be a nice young man."

"Thank you, Mrs. Williams." Sarah was very happy to hear those words and there was no longer any need to worry about Josh being in school. "I'm glad that you feel that way. I was afraid that you might have some problems with him being in school," Sarah told her.

Mrs. Williams sipped her coffee. "I would have had a problem if you had not put him in school. If anyone has a problem with Josh being in school, I want you to talk with me."

Sarah was now relieved.

Josh had a nice time in school. When the day was over, he took the long way home walking along the path down by the creek, near the area where he had walked many times with his mother. It was the beginning of his love for nature. In the past, when they went for walks, he and his mother would pick flowers. He knew not why his mother picked flowers then but now he was picking them for her.

His mother was a bit concerned about him being a little late coming home, but when he showed up with a bow of flowers, she was happy to see him standing there. Mrs. Williams smiled when she saw him sitting on a bench in the kitchen with his mother. She thought of the day when her granddaughter would also be coming home from school.

"What did you do in school today?" asked Sarah, admiring the flowers as she placed her nose close to the blossom so she could smell the aroma.

"We talked about the alphabets." Josh was excited, talking about his teacher. "Mr. Smith said that he was going to teach us how to read and write," Josh said with a grin on his face.

"Do you like the teacher?" Sarah asked.

"Yes," Josh said. "He's a good guy. He likes animals and plants and talked about all kinds of things today." Josh added as he pointed to the flowers that he had brought to his mother. "These flowers are daffodils."

Sarah was impressed. "They are beautiful, thanks for bringing them to me." Wanting to finish the day, Sarah asked, "Josh, do you think that you can go home and study your schoolwork while I work here?"

"Yes, Mom, I'll be okay."

She instructed him to call if he needed anything and watched as her son got ready to go home.

Josh picked up his schoolwork and walked 150 yards to his house. It was the first time that they had been separated, but she could see her house from the window of the kitchen in the big house. Sarah was comfortable with him being there.

By the time Josh turned nine, Josh was doing very well in school. Mr. Jones had learned that he loved animals and gave Josh a couple of biddies to raise. Josh did not think of them as pets. To him, they were livestock so he built a pen to keep them in. He was proud of his biddies, and often spoke of them in class. Mr. Smith saw that the children were all interested in Josh's hobby so he used it as a subject in his classroom.

By the third year, the school's students had doubled. The parents had found that their children were interested in learning so they made every effort to send them to school. The landowners, however, thought that they all should be in the fields working. Most thought that a black child had no need for education. The only thing that they were expected to do was work in the fields and they did not need to read or write to do that.

One day, Mr. Smith was on a field trip with his class and some of the white men saw him with the class and reported it to the county commissioners, saying that the kids were playing in the fields instead of being taught in the classroom. Some even tried to make a rule that a boy ten years old or older be required to work with their father as part of the sharecropper contract, but the rule failed. Sarah had gotten no opposition from the Williamses so she continued to send Josh to school.

One day, Josh and the rest of his schoolmates were sitting in class when a carload of KKK members drove by the school and angrily screamed. "Close the school and go home!" Mr. Smith said nothing. He just sat there shaking. As the men approached, he got up and went to the door.

Continuing their threats, they warned the teacher and his class. "Get out of here and go home while you can."

That day, Josh ran straight home. Crying, he wondered why the masked men had come into their school. His mind was confused. "Why did they scare, Mr. Smith? Why did they make us leave the school?" He ran into the kitchen screaming for his mother. "Why! Why!" he cried. "Why did they make Mr. Smith leave?"

Sarah tried to calm her son. "Who? she asked. Sarah rubbed Josh's hands. "Who made the teacher leave?"

Josh was inconsolable. "The men in the hoods! They made Mr. Smith leave. He was so scared. He was trembling." Josh began to cry again. "They yelled at him, Mama, and made him leave."

Sarah hugged her boy. She could feel the pains, remembering how she felt when the clan came for Bert.

"Hush! Hush!" she said, trying to calm him down. "It's going to be all right. Everything is going to be all right." She kept telling her child, not knowing what the clan would do.

Josh's sobs calmed a bit. Still, his body trembled and tears ran down his cheeks.

Mrs. Williams, who was in her living room, had heard the commotion coming from the kitchen. She was concerned and when she heard the word *clan*, she called for Sarah. "What's going on with Josh? What's he crying about?"

Sarah held Josh. "Some men came to the school," Sarah said. "They ran Mr. Smith away. Josh said that they had masks on. I think they must be the clan."

Mrs. Williams shook her head in shame.

Mr. Williams was growing weaker from his illness, but when Mrs. Williams told him what had happened at the school, he forced himself to go to the parish seat to see if he could get the commissioners to get Mr. Smith back into the classroom. Later, he could see that the trip and the aggregation of dealing with people in the parish seat was causing him to become weaker so he started to make plans to have a good talk with his son about the business of running the plantation.

Junior was on his way home and had decided to stop at a restaurant for a drink. One of the men in the place came over and sat down beside him. "I hear that your father went to the county commissioners and asked them to reopen the black school," the man said.

"I did not know that the school was closed," Junior said. He had no idea what was going on at the school nor did he know why his father would go to the parish seat to discuss it.

"They say that it will be opened as soon as the teacher returns."

Junior was concerned. "What if the teacher does not return?"

"They are going to get a new teacher, I'm told."

Junior downed his drink. "Well, that was a legal school. No one has the right to interfere with the school or the students."

While he held his ground with the man at the bar, he wondered what his father had done and why the man was telling him about it.

As Junior approached the house, he saw Marge sitting on the front porch reading to their daughter, Brenda. He loved his family and kissed Marge when he reached her.

Marge was concerned about her husband knowing his father was short on time and wondered how he would react to the bad news when it came. She kissed her husband and said, "Your dad said that he wanted to have a talk with you," pointing to the living room.

Junior was apprehensive whenever he spoke to his father. This was one of those times. "So what's going on?" he asked. He was preparing to hear the news, whatever the news was.

Mr. Williams was direct. "Well, son, you know a man was not born to live forever and the doctors seem to think that I may not be here too much longer. That will leave you here to take care of your mother and this place." Mr. Williams was deep in thought. "I've been thinking for some time now that freeing of the slaves might not have been such a bad idea."

Junior tried to understand what his father was trying to say but needed him to get to the point. "Dad, what are you saying?

"I'm saying that they are people just like everyone else. Once you work with them a while, you'll get to see that. It first came to me some years ago when I saw Bert stand up to the clan. I could see it in his eyes. There was a man standing there before me and he was not white."

Mr. Williams stood up as if he was proud to have made that statement, then he said, "That's why I told them downtown that they should reopen the school and keep it open. He looked into his son's eyes and said, "I want you to treat the tenants on this place fair. If you do, I believe that you will have a good life and be glad that you did."

Mr. Williams passed away two weeks after his talk with his son. It was also his granddaughter's birthday. Robert Williams Jr. was the one who would miss the old man the most. He had heard what his father had to say even when it seemed that he was not listening. Mrs. Williams would sometimes catch herself smiling when she thought she heard her husband, but it was her son instead of the old man.

It took Mr. Smith some time to get himself together and open the school for class again. Josh spent most of his time after school, working with his chickens and two ducks that another man had given him for his ninth birthday.

Mr. Smith had been a student at Tuskegee Institute. He used his knowledge of what blacks were doing to encourage the students to look forward to doing more than farming.

The new tenant who had moved into Sarah's old house had a daughter named Alice. Alice was two years younger than Josh. She, Josh, and another young girl named Ellie Mae soon began to walk to and from school together. The parents of the three students from Swamp Town encouraged them to walk together for safety's sake, knowing that there were lots of crazy people in the area. This togetherness created a great friendship between the three of them. Sometimes, they would stop by Josh's house and play with the animals that Josh had in his backyard.

He now had six chickens, three ducks, and a dog. While his neighbors had given him wire to build a pen to keep the animals in, the rest of the materials he had gathered for himself.

Junior's daughter, Brenda, was nine years old and her father thought that it would be nice for her to have a swimming pool. Building the swimming pool for her was just an excuse. He had always wanted a pool for himself, but it would also be nice for Brenda and her friends.

Brenda's friend Grace lived in the big house down the lane from the Williamses. Her father, Mr. Peterson, was the banker in Baton Rouge. He was a short man, who stood about five feet six inches, a bald man who had to comb his hair over the top of his head to give the illusion of having hair. He was always dressed well and liked a good cigar.

Because of the two girls, who would often play together, were friends, Junior figured that this would be a good way to have a good connection with one of the biggest bankers in town. After a few weeks, Junior met the banker in Baton Rouge and made arrangements to have a swimming pool built on his property. The construction plans showed a sixteen-by-thirty-foot pool with enough patio space for lawn chairs and a small house for changing into swimming suits. While doing business with the banker, they soon became friends as he had planned.

Josh observed the pool's construction and was amazed at the big machinery that was being used to dig this big hole and to see how easily it could move such large amounts of dirt. In the evenings, after he came home from school, he would stand at the edge of the yard and watch the men work with amazement and wonder.

Early one evening, Josh met his mother at the door, excited at what he was seeing. He called his mother and said excitedly, "Mama, did you see that big thing out there in the yard?"

"Yes, I saw it," his mother said. Josh was very excited, watching the men working on the swimming pool. Sarah wanted to rest from the day but was always ready to encourage Josh in his eagerness to learn.

"What is it?" asked Josh.

"I don't know," she said." Why don't you ask your teacher tomorrow? I'm sure he can tell you what it is."

Josh went to bed that night, eager to speak to Mr. Smith the next day. As he entered the school that morning, he immediately ran to his teacher's desk. With excitement, he asked Mr. Smith what that big thing in the Williams's yard was.

"Do you mean that big yellow machine?" Mr. Smith asked. He was happy to see Josh's enthusiasm.

"Yes, sir," Josh said.

"That thing is called a backhoe. It is used for digging holes."

Josh's eyes widened. He was even more fascinated.

The next day, Mr. Smith told his class that he had a surprise for them. They were going on a field trip. "Josh has told me that he saw a machine that most of us in this neighborhood have never seen, so we are going to see it," he told them.

That following day, Mr. Smith took his eager class down to the work site so that they could see how the backhoe was used. At this point, the workmen had brought in another machine. Mr. Smith, who never missed an opportunity to teach, said to his students, "Do you see that other machine there by that large pile of dirt?"

They replied with an excited "Yes!"

"That's called a front-end loader," he said. "Now watch and see how easily it is able to put all of that dirt into the truck in a very short amount of time."

His students, especially Josh, were amazed at how much those machines could do in such a short period of time.

That evening, Josh went to his mother and told her what Mr. Smith had shown his class.

Sarah loved seeing her son so engaged. "Did you enjoy it?" she asked.

"I enjoyed it very much," Josh replied. "Do you think that I could learn to drive one of those machines?

Sarah touched her son gently. "Of course, you can. You can do anything anyone else can do."

Josh was happy. "That's what I want to do when I grow up," he told his mother.

Sarah assured her son. "You just keep studying hard in school and you will be able to drive that machine and more."

It took about three months to complete the pool. Junior invited the banker's daughter and several other white children of the neighborhood to come over for a swim. Josh sat there on the front porch of his house knowing that he was not wanted. Feeling rejected, he went around to the rear of his house where he could not be seen. He could not understand why he was not accepted. His skin was nearly as white as theirs; his hair was the same. He sat there alone wondering what he had done. He later took a slow walk down to one of the black neighbor's house where a young boy named Jack lived. Josh and Jack went for a walk down by the creek.

They were both skipping rocks across the creek when Jack asked, "Did they ever get that pool finish?"

Josh looked solemn. "Yeah, but we can't swim in it," he said.

"You know we can't swim in it, Josh. We're black," said Jack.

Josh looked at him. "I'm not black," Josh said.

"Yes, you are," Jack replied. "You don't look black, but you are black."

Josh realized what his friend meant. Jack could see Josh's mind thinking. Wanting to change the subject, he looked at the water. "Have you ever been down here to do any fishing?" Jack asked.

No," said Josh. He picked up a pebble and threw it across the creek. "But I love to come down here to sit and watch the animals that live around the water."

"Me too," said Jack. "I really like being alone out here, but I don't mind being with you."

Absentmindedly, Josh picked up a rock. "Why don't you go to school?" he asked his friend.

"I work in the field with my father. He needs us to help him chop the fields." Jack was sad about this, but he had to do what he had to do.

"You should ask your father to let you go to school with me." Josh wanted to help his friend. "We learn lots of thing at the school."

"I'm twelve years old," Jack said. "What good would it do for me to go to that school?" For a few minutes, they were silent. They sat there and watched the water rippling each time a frog jumped in or one of them threw a rock in the creek. There was not much being said now, but they were very comfortable in each other's company.

The two boys spent the rest of the day at the creek's edge, exploring their own world. When they left the creek, they walked down the path that went past the house where Bert used to live. When they came to the barn that housed the livestock, the new tenant was sitting on the fence just like Bert used to do and Alice was sitting in the front yard, playing with her grass dolls. Josh waved at her. "I'll see you in school Monday, Alice," he said.

She glanced up from her dolls for a moment. "See you Monday," she replied. Jack said his good-byes and started up the dirt road to his home.

It was quiet now. Josh could not hear the excitement of the girls playing in the pool. Anyone could see that he was upset. He did not understand why he, who lived next door to the pool, was not invited to go for a swim in this brand new pool. When Sarah came in and saw him sitting at the table not saying a word, she did not bother to ask why he had been out so long. She knew why he was feeling left out and she understood. She knew she would have to speak to him at some point. Now was not the time.

The youngest son of Ray Jones had been doing part-time work for the Williamses. The work consisted of keeping the yard clean and keeping plenty of wood chopped for cooking and keeping the house warm. The job was now open because Ben had gotten married and moved to Baton Rouge. Junior asked Josh if he would like to have the job. Josh quickly said yes.

He was fourteen years old when he started working for the Williamses. When he got home from school, he would do his homework and then go to the Williams's house and start cutting wood. After he had finished cutting the wood, he'd take it to the back porch and stacked it neatly just outside the door of the kitchen where his mother worked. This was good for the both of them because he was still welcomed in the kitchen and the work kept him busy. The job also included cleaning the area around the pool. He made sure that when he got to that job, none of the youngsters would be there to jeer at him.

Josh was growing up to become quite a handsome young man. His walking back and forth from school, going for long walks, and swimming in the creek along with cutting wood was beginning to show in the muscular build of his body. He was over five feet tall and weighed about 150 pounds.

Josh and Jack were best friends now. They often talked of the things that Josh learned in school. One of the things that Jack was most interested in was a man named George Washington Carver, and according to Josh, there was a great deal to be said about that man.

Mr. Smith had said so much about the man, George Washington Carver, that Josh talked as if he knew him. The two friends were walking along the dirt road as they had done many times before Josh kept on talking about this man, telling Jack of all the things that people were saying about him. Josh could see that Jack was very interested in learning and knew that he longed to be in school.

This was one of those days when the two of them enjoyed just walking along this dirt road enjoying each other's friendship. "A lot of things are going on at Tuskegee," Josh told Jack.

"What kind of other things do they do at this school?" Jack asked. He was walking along with a stick, making waves in the water of the gully. Every now and then, he'd hit the water, trying to dislodge a minnow from the gully.

"Do you mean Tuskegee?" Josh asked. "They do lots of things there." While they talked, Josh was walking on the edge of the field, picking up rocks, and throwing them at the birds.

"Like what?" Jack asked.

"They say, that they teach young men how to fly airplanes," Josh said as he threw a rock across the field.

Jack stopped. "No they don't," he said. "Black men can't fly airplanes."

Josh looked at his friend. "Mr. Smith said that they do and he went to that school," Josh replied.

"Have you ever seen an airplane?" asked Jack. He was intrigued.

"No! But I've seen a zeppelin," Josh said while watching the birds flutter in a bush on a ditch bank.

Interested, Jack sat on the creek's edge. "What is a zeppelin?"

"It's a big balloon-like thing that floats around up in the air."

"Boy, I sure would like to see one of those things. Do you think black men can fly one of those zeppelins?"

Josh replied with a smile, "Mr. Smith says some of them can." With that, they got up and started walking away from the creek.

"Boy, I sure would like to fly one of those things," said Jack. "It must be fun." The two boys walked all the way down to Jesse Mae's place, walking and talking about the exciting things Josh had learned in school. Upon reaching Jessie Mae's place, Josh and Jack bought cold drinks and continued to dream of how they would like to learn to fly airplanes.

That following Monday, when Josh got to school, he spoke to Mr. Smith about how he and Jack had discussed his class on how black men were being trained to be pilots. Mr. Smith asked Josh to invite Jack to come to the school and sit in on one of his classes. That afternoon, Josh told Jack what Mr. Smith had said.

One day, when Jack had no work to do on the farm, he walked down to the school. Josh and Mr. Smith had forgotten that they had invited Jack to come to school to hear some of the things that went on at Tuskegee, but Josh was very happy that his friend had shown up.

Jack was standing at the door. He had never been in a school before and his nerves were telling on him. Josh got up from his seat, walked over to Jack, and introduced him as his friend. For the remainder of that class, Mr. Smith spoke about the many things that he had taught his students. He spoke of men who flew airplanes and studied science and taught math. When Mr. Smith was finished, he invited Jack to come again.

That evening, Josh came home and found his mother standing at the woodpile. He was surprised to see her there. "What are you doing out here?" he asked.

"I want to talk to you before Mr. Williams has to talk to you," she told him.

"What's wrong?"

His mother was stern. "Mr. Williams is paying you to keep plenty of wood cut for the kitchen and the house. You are to keep as much stacked on the porch as was there when you started the job. Look around," Sarah motioned "This pile is getting smaller. A good worker looks ahead and make sure that things are done before he has to be told."

Josh did not like to see his mother angry. "Yeah, Ma, I know what you're saying and why you're saying it." He picked up his ax and went to work. He chopped wood for the rest of the afternoon and stacked it on the back porch until he was sure that he had more than the amount that was there when he had started the job. He did not understand why she spoke to him about following the rules of keeping up with his work but he understood why.

Josh had just finished stacking the wood and sat down to take a break when Brenda approached him out of nowhere. She had been watching him work and wanted a chance to talk with him.

Looking for a conversation with him, she walked up to him and said, "Hello, Josh. What are you doing?"

"Getting some wood together for the house," Josh said.

She sat on the bottom step. "Are you still going to that black school?"

Josh looked at her oddly. "Yeah, that's the only school that I have to go to."

Brenda seemed nervous. "Why don't you come to my pool some time?"

Josh was astonished by the offer. "You know that I can't go to your pool."

"Why not?"

Josh looked at her with a pause. "Because I'm black," he said. He was becoming irritated at her for asking why he had not been at her pool when she had not invited him. So he walked away.

CHAPTER 6

MRS. WILLIAMS HAD seen the two of them talking, so she decided to have a talk with Brenda, but first she would talk with her mother. When Marge came home, she saw that her mother-in-law wanted to talk. She flopped down on the couch, kicking her shoes off her tired feet, and asked her mother-in-law what was going on.

"Well, there's no need beating around the bush," Mrs. Williams said. "I saw Brenda talking to Josh today. You know, the people in this area won't think much of a black boy talking to a white girl."

"Yeah, I know," Marge said. "But what can we do?" Marge's feet was aching earlier and now, so was her head.

"We have got to talk to her and let her know why things are like they are. It's going to be up to us to stop this in the bud," Mrs. Williams said.

Marge did not want to deal with the drama. "You know these people better than I do," Marge said. "Would you talk to her for me?"

Mrs. Williams said, "I'd be glad to."

When Brenda came in from school that afternoon, her grandmother asked to speak with her. Brenda ran upstairs, threw her books on the bed, and bounced back down stairs.

"It's about Josh," Mrs. Williams was serious. "You know that the white people in this neighborhood don't like the idea of blacks and whites going together.

Brenda was shocked. "What's the problem, Grandma? I only spoke to him."

Gently, her grandmother tried to explain. "I know, but if people see you talking to him, they'll get crazy ideas and we don't want that, do we?"

Brenda did not understand. "I don't see anything wrong with talking to somebody. What has he done so wrong that we can't be friends?"

"He's done nothing girl. It's this world that's all screwed up, so please listen to me this one time and be careful. Your actions could get him killed." Brenda didn't say a word. She just got up from her seat and walked upstairs. She laid there on her bed, trying to understand what her grandmother had said, and why just talking to Josh could cause him to lose his life.

Later that evening, Brenda's mind was still confused. She decided to get up and go for a walk, but she would not take the chance of going by Josh's house for fear that she might be seen near him. She headed toward her friend Grace's house. She could talk to Grace. Grace would help her understand.

She walked down to the gates that lead up to Grace's house. She could see Grace sitting in a swing on her porch, so she stopped at the gate.

"Grace!" She yelled from the gate.

Grace looked up and saw her friend. "Hey! How are you doing, Brenda?"

"I'm fine, just going for a walk."

Grace could tell that her friend was upset by the sound of her voice. "Come on up and have a seat," Grace said, sliding over on the swing to make room for her.

Brenda did not move. "No, come and go for a walk with me."

Grace placed the book that she was reading on a table next to the swing and walked down to the gate where Brenda was waiting. They walked down the road toward the general store.

As they strolled, Grace could see that her friend was in a bad mood. "You seem upset, girl. What's up?"

Brenda was in deep thought. "What do you mean?"

"You don't seem to be your happy self."

"I'm all right," Brenda said. Then she hesitated before saying, "I just had this crazy conversation with my grandma."

Grace, casually strolling along, asked, "What were you two talking about?"

"She wanted to know why I was talking to Josh," Brenda said.

Grace was surprised. "You were talking to Josh? What were you too talking about?"

"It was nothing." Brenda replied. "I just spoke to him and asked him why he didn't come over and play in the pool with us."

Grace stopped in her tracks. "What did he say?"

"He said that he was not allowed to play in the pool with us."

"Why did you ask him that? You knew that he couldn't play in the pool with us because he's black." Grace was surprised that Brenda didn't know that.

Brenda was firm. "What if he was my friend?"

Grace tried to be sympathetic. "That doesn't make any difference, he's black." Grace said, and shook her head. "Honey, you have got a lot to learn."

The two girls walked about three quarters of a mile from Grace's father's farm before walking into the corner drugstore. The two of them ordered an ice cream soda and sat there listening to the jukebox playing their favorite tune. The two of them would normally be happy in a place like this, but today the subject had spoiled their mood.

It was late in the summer, the year of Brenda's sixteenth birthday. She was now dating David, the son of the drugstore owner. David was a young man, blond with blue eyes, about five feet eight inches tall, and about 160 pounds. Brenda had invited David, her two girlfriends, and the girls' dates over for a swim. The six of them were having fun at the pool. The three girls were relaxed in their lawn chairs while the boys were swimming laps, racing each other in the pool.

Grace pulled her lawn chair over close to where Brenda and her other friend were sitting and whispered, "Have you seen Josh lately?"

"No," Brenda said softly. "We don't discuss that subject around here."

Just as she finished her sentence, David climbed out of the pool and asked, "What subject?"

Brenda heard him but said nothing.

Doris, one of the girls who cane with David's friend, chimed in saying, "They were talking about someone named Josh."

David was not amused. "Who's Josh?" David asked.

Brenda looked at Doris and rolled her eyes. "That's a closed subject," she replied.

David asked, "Is he someone you have been seeing behind my back?"

"You must be crazy," Brenda replied angrily. "You don't own me. I will talk to whomever I please! No one is going to tell me who I can talk to." Her anger had increased because now it was her boyfriend who was telling her who she could talk to. After her outburst, she got up and left the pool.

Before Brenda's guests left the pool, Grace told David that Mrs. Williams had spoken to Brenda about talking to Josh and that Josh was the black boy who worked for them. David was upset at Brenda's reaction because he thought of her as being his steady. He wanted to speak to Brenda before he left, but she went into the house closing the door behind her with a slam. Brenda did not wish to speak to him or anyone else. Angrily, he climbed out of the pool and sped away in his car with a cloud of dust trailing behind him. In his eagerness to find out who this Josh was, David stopped by Jesse Mae's place to ask about him.

Jesse Mae was somewhat concerned when she saw David speeding toward her place. He drove up and shouted out, "Where is Josh?"

Jesse Mae could see the anger in the boy's eyes.

"Who wants to know?" said Jesse Mae, who was not moved by his boldness.

"I'm Brenda's boyfriend," he said.

Jesse Mae slowly walked over to David's car. She looked into his eyes and said, "Josh is my friend. You can tell me what you want with him."

"Why should I tell you anything," David asked.

"Because I don't want my friend to get into any trouble for killing you," she replied. With that, she turned and walked slowly back into her place. David cranked his car and drove slowly toward his father's store.

Jesse Mae sent her son to tell Josh what had just happened. "And tell him that I know that he has what he needs to take care of himself," speaking of the pistol that Bert has left him.

Josh was back on his job the next week as if nothing had happened. Brenda walked past him in the backyard and did not say a word. This angered him, but he did not say a word either. His rage was boiling in his heart, but he knew nothing that she had done. It was as if he was angry with the world but had no place to direct that anger.

Josh continued to cut wood as he was hired to do, his woodpile increased far beyond what it would normally be on a normal day, but he had not piled it on the back porch as he should have done. Now as Brenda walked past him without saying a word, he could see that he still had a monumental job of neatly piling the wood as his mother had told him to do.

Josh did get his job completed, but instead of going into the kitchen and talking to his mother for a few moments, he just went home and tried to relax his mind. He sat there in his house, trying to understand why anyone would get so upset because someone had spoken to him and now why would she come out here and not speak? He was very confused. The only thing that he could see that he had done was to tell Brenda why he could not talk to her. When he realized that he was not alone, he looked up and his friend Jack was standing in the doorway.

"What's up?" Jack was saying. Josh relaxed. "I was just sitting here trying to get my mind together."

"I've heard about what's been going on with you," Jack said as he walked inside with Josh.

"Yeah, I don't understand it. I have not done anything to anyone and people want to hurt me."

"You know that you are going to have to watch you back, don't you?"

"Yeah, man," Josh told him. "And when I'm alone, I want to be alone."

Jack knew that Josh needed to be safe from his enemies. "You got protection?" he asked.

"Daddy Bert left me some protection when he died," Josh told him.

"Good," Jack said. "Then I want have to leave you anything," speaking of the gun that he had intended to leave with Josh if he needed it.

Josh was grateful. "Thanks a lot," he said. "You are a good friend." Jack tucked the gift that he had brought over for Josh back into his belt and headed back to his house.

It was getting close to the end of the school year. Brenda was getting ready for graduation from the white school while Josh was getting ready for graduation from the black school. Josh was about to turn eighteen and Brenda's seventeenth birthday was just two weeks away.

Josh had walked to and from school with Alice every day since she had started school. They had always been friends, but Josh had never thought of her as being his girlfriend.

It was a few days before school was to close for the summer and this was to be Josh's last day there. He met Alice at the end of the lane where he had met her every day since he had started walking her to school. He had always liked her, but he had never seen what a beautiful girl she was. Alice was a nice girl and Josh liked that. Josh was now really seeing this person for the first time, and he liked the little things that he may not have even noticed had he not liked her. Her movements were slow and graceful even though she did not have the long slender legs that were normally associated with such graceful movements. Her eyes seemed normal at first, but when she talked, they rolled and moved in a sensual way.

Alice could talk to Josh. Sometimes, she would open up with things that he believed she would hesitate to tell anyone else. Because of her openness with him, he felt that he knew her. So easy was she to talk to that he would confide in her, knowing that whatever he told her, she would keep it confidential. It was that day on their way home from school that he asked her to be his girl. She smiled with the smile of the school-age girl that she was and said, "Josh, I'll always be your girl."

That evening, after Josh walked Alice home, all was well with the world. He went to the woodpile and chopped wood with an excessive amount of energy. Later, he went into the kitchen where his mother was, hugged her, and then kissed her on the cheek.

"What are you so happy about?" his mother asked.

"I feel good," he said.

"Come on, Josh. What are you so happy about?" she asked him again.

With a grin on his face, he looked at his mother and said, "You know that girl that I've been walking to school with?" Without hesitation, he shouted out, "I asked Alice to be my girl."

"What did she say?" his mother asked.

"She said 'yes.'"

That afternoon, Jack decided to walk down to Josh's house, and as he approached the house, he saw Josh in the backyard feeding his chickens. Josh had started with two biddies and now he had a variety of animals at his place. Josh was proud of his animals. He now had twenty chicken, ten ducks, and six guinea fowls that he kept in a pen. The birds laid lots of eggs that he sold to Jesse Mae or gave to some of his neighbors if they needed them.

Jack was in a bit of a hurry that afternoon and needed to ask his friend a question before he continued to his destination.

"Hello," Jack said to Josh as he approached him in his backyard.

As Josh turned to face Jack, he still had a smile on his face.

"What's going on with you?" Jack asked.

"Nothing."

"It can't be nothing. A man don't smile like that for nothing."

"Maybe…It just maybe that I'm smiling because I just asked Alice to be my girl," he said as his smile increased to cover his entire face. Josh could see that his friend was not smiling with him. "What's wrong, Jack?"

"I guess I just lost again," Jack said, but I'm glad that this time, I lost to a friend.

"What are you talking about, Jack?"

"I came to ask you if you thought that I should ask Alice If she would be my girl."

"I'm sorry, Jack. I'm so sorry. I hope that we can still be friends."

"This doesn't change our friendship, Josh. We'll always be friends." After hesitating for a few seconds, Jack said, "I'm going to that place where those black guys fly those airplanes and see if I can get me a job there." The statement that Jack had made had come from nowhere. It may have been that he wanted to get away or it may have been that he wanted a place to let his heart heal.

"That is a good idea," said Josh. "I'll go and talk to Mr. Smith tomorrow and ask him if he'll write you a letter of introduction."

"Thank you," Jack said, saying good-bye as he walked away.

Josh had mixed feelings as he watched his friend walk away. He thought that this may be the last time that he would see his friend. Later that evening, he walked down to Jesse Mae's place. He did not realize it, but he walked over and sat in the seat where Bert used to sit. When Jesse Mae saw that, the memory of Bert made chills run down her back.

Before she realized it, Jesse had walked over and sat down beside him just as she had done many times with Bert. She looked at Josh, thinking of Bert. "What's going on with you?" she asked.

Josh asked for a drink and sighed. "I'm feeling good and bad at the same time." Unconsciously, he tapped his finger on the table as if he was trying to figure something out.

"That sounds a little bit impossible," Jesse said. "But tell me about it."

"You know my friend Jack," Josh said.

Jesse nodded.

"He's talking about leaving the area. I'm going to miss him." He sighed again. "He's my best friend."

Jesse, trying to make him feel better, said, "That's not so bad. You will see him every now and then."

"I told him that I had told Alice that I wanted her to be my girlfriend and that she had said yes."

Jesse knew that there was more to the story. "What's so bad about that?" Jesse Mae asked.

Josh could not look in her eyes when he quietly said, "He wanted her to be his girlfriend."

"Oh, Lord," Jesse Mae said. "That's rough." Seeing the sad look on his face, she took a deep breath trying to compose herself.

"We are still friends," said Josh as he got up and walked out of the door.

The next day, he went to see his teacher Mr. Smith and asked him to give Jack a letter of introduction.

Chapter 7

About two weeks after Jack last saw his friend Josh, he went by the school and picked up the letter. The letter was there just as Josh had said it would be. The letter was in an envelope—inside a larger envelope. Mr. Smith told Jack to remove the smaller letter from the larger one and give the smaller envelope to a Mr. Jacob when he got to Tuskegee.

Jack, who had never been out of Swamp Town, was now on his way to Tuskegee, a place that he had only heard of in a class of elementary school students. He had heard that Tuskegee was in a place called Alabama but had no idea how to get there. After speaking with Mr. Smith, the next day, he got on a bus in Baton Rouge and rode until he got to a place called Montgomery, Alabama. He then was to ask the clerk at that bus station about a bus that goes to Tuskegee.

Jack's instructions were clear, but he had no idea that the trip would take so long. The back of the bus was crowded with no place to sleep. He had a burlap bag with his extra clothes and some food that his mother had cooked for him. The bus driver had insisted that all the black passengers be crammed in a smaller and smaller space as more and more white passengers got on board the bus.

The trip was uncomfortable and you had to go to the back door of the bus station if you wanted to purchase some food or to get any information that you needed. Jack, who had lived in Swamp Town all of his life, had no idea what the real world was like. He was a bit timid about asking the clerk in Montgomery for information about how to get to Tuskegee but was surprised about how pleasant the clerk was.

Later, while on the bus, Jack started wondering why Mr. Smith had given him two envelopes. Mr. Smith had said to give Mr. Jacob the inner envelope so he felt that he had the right to open the outer one. When he opened it, a twenty-dollar bill fell out of it. Now he knew that Mr. Smith was giving him some financial help, and this was twice the amount of what he had in his pocket. He was now sure that the Lord was taking care of him.

When Jack arrived at Tuskegee's bus station, he was met by a man who walked up to him and asked if he was Jack Tyson.

"I'm Jack Tyson," Jack replied. The man introduced himself as Ralph Jacob and told Jack that Mr. Smith had asked him to meet Jack there.

Jack was overwhelmed. "Thank you…thank you very much, sir," he told Mr. Jacob. "I had no idea what I was going to do."

Mr. Jacob looked the young man over. "Well, young man," he said, "I understand that you are in need of a job."

"I am, sir," Jack said.

"What do you like to do?" Mr. Jacob asked. He was trying to get to know Jack and to see what he was willing to do.

"I'll do any job that I can get," said Jack, who was eager to get anything that was offered.

"The job I have is cleaning the workshop," Mr. Jacob told Jack.

"I am very thankful and I'll do a good job, you'll see." Jack told him.

Mr. Jacob liked the young man immediately. "I believe you will, Jack. I believe you will."

Jack piled his bag of belongings into the back of Mr. Jacob's Model T Ford and they headed toward Mr. Jacob's place. The trip was about twenty-five miles through dirt roads in mostly empty countryside. They pulled into a driveway of a large white two-story house and drove through the front yard and around two large magnolia trees then continued around the house to a smaller building with a set of double door at the ground level and an outside stairway that led up to the second floor.

Mr. Jacob parked the car in front of the double doors of the smaller building, and said, "You'll be staying in this building. There's a room upstairs with a bed. You can see the outhouse over there and there is a pump inside the shop on the lower level. The two people who work in the shop will be here from Monday through Saturday. Your job will be to keep the shop clean. There will be other things for you to do later, but for now, just concentrate on the shop."

He could tell that Jack was exhausted. "I know that you're tired," Mr. Jacob said, "so why don't you take your things upstairs and get some rest."

Jack had never been happier. "Thank you, sir," Jack said. "Thank you very much."

Upstairs in Jack's room, in addition to the bed, there was a small table, chair, and a foot tub. Jack was so tired that he flopped down on the bed and was asleep before his head hit the pillow. He woke up two hours later from hearing a knock on the door downstairs. "Who is it?" he asked. Jack looked down from the second floor of the shop and saw a lady standing there.

"I'm Mrs. Jacobs," the lady said. "You're going to eat with us until you get yourself situated. We'll be ready in fifteen minutes. Come to the kitchen when you're ready."

Mr. Jacob was one of the teachers at Tuskegee. He had taught Mr. Smith and his son was one of the trainee pilots. At dinner, Mr. Jacob told Jack all about what was going on at the site, what Jack's job would be, and who he would be working for. Mrs. Jacob mentioned that their son was away for a while and would be home in a few weeks.

Their son Billy was just two years older than Jack and had completed high school and was now in college. Jack thought, *How could it be that in Swamp Town no black person had even considered completing high school, while here in this place, black people were completing college.* That moment, Jack decided that he could do better for himself.

After dinner was over, Jack offered to help Mrs. Jacob with the dishes.

"No," she said. "Just go take a walk, look around, and make yourself at home. You'll have plenty of work to do starting Monday morning."

That Monday morning, Mr. Jacob took Jack for a ride around the property. They went out to the landing strip. There were two small aircrafts parked at the far end of the field. As they drove around, Mr. Jacob told Jack a little about the history of the place. There were all types of questions in Jack's mind. His curiosity finally got the best of him, so he asked the question that had been on his mind for some time now.

"Sir, how can black men learn to fly things like that?" he said as he pointed toward the airplanes.

Mr. Jacob spoke to the eager young man, saying, "You've got a lot to learn." Then he added, "A black man is the same as any other man. He can learn and do what any other man can do." Then he asked, "Did you ever hear of a poem that a man wrote about what a man is?"

Jack listened intently. "No, sir." Jack was embarrassed. He didn't want to say it but out it came, "I can't read, sir. Tell me what the poem says."

Mr. Jacob could see that Jack needed and wanted more. "Would you like to learn to read?" Mr. Jacob asked.

"I sure would," Jack said with happiness in his voice. "I surely would."

"The poem went something like this," said Mr. Jacob.

A man is a man and what he is,
He is that and that alone.
Nothing more,
Nothing less.
For what is a man, except
What he is?
If he tries to be more than what he is, he fails.
If he settles for less than what he is,
He is not a man.
Be therefore, all that you are,
Until there is nothing left.
For it is such a simple task,
Just be yourself.

Jack was amazed. "I like that," he said. "Can you teach me to read something like that?"

"Yes," Mr. Jacob replied.

"Who did you say wrote that?" Jack was interested in finding out if it was a black man.

"His name is James P. Daniels. He is a friend of mine."

"Is he a black man?"

"Yes."

Mr. Jacob took Jack to a small barn where he kept a horse and a grass mower. "One of the jobs that you will be doing is mowing the airstrip. Do you think you can do that?"

"No problem," said Jack. "I have seen how these things work."

Mr. Jacob then took his new helper back to the shop. The older man took the long way back so that Jack could see the layout of the place. Jack was amazed at how much property these people had.

On the edges of the place were small gardens and fruit trees. Beyond the property line, he could see people working in the fields, chopping and plowing their crops. As they approached the shop where he would be working, he saw several men standing around an airplane that had been moved to the area and the engine was still running. These new sights and sounds made him feel very proud and the look in his face showed it.

Mr. Jacob drove up to the shop and introduced him to the people that he would be working with. Two of the men were trainee pilots. The other two were mechanics. Jack had a good feeling about this job. There was so much that he could learn and he was so eager to learn it. Jack got out of the car and followed Mr. Jacob to where the men stood.

"Good morning," Mr. Jacob said. "This is our new man, Jack."

The men gave Jack a once over. "Hello, Jack," The men said in unison.

Jack exchanged pleasantries. He was glad to be there. The men came over to him and shook his hand. Jack had a very good feeling about the friendliness of the men and the feeling kept getting better and better. Mr. Jacob had called him their new man and now all of these men were shaking his hand. The youngest pilot was called Jim; the older one was called Fred. Then there was Jake; he was the oldest of them all. Young Jim told Jack that it was time to eat.

Mrs. Jacob had brought food for all of the men and it was placed on a table near Jim's workbench. As the men gathered around, it was clear that this was the beginning of a new friendship.

CHAPTER 8

JOSH HAD JUST completed cleaning the yard and had decided to saw some of the logs into smaller pieces. Because the logs were delivered to the woodpile in ten-foot sections, Josh had to cut them into shorter pieces so that he split them.

Alice's father, Jake, had come over to help Josh load the logs onto the racks so that they could be sawed into eighteen-inch sections.

"Mr. Williams asked me to come over and help you with the logs," Jake told Josh. "With us working together, the job will be much easier."

"Thank you," said Josh. "I do need and appreciate the help."

"You are becoming quite a young man," said Jake as he watched Josh lift those logs as if they were not heavy at all. "How old are you now?"

"I'll be eighteen my birthday."

They worked on the pile of logs for the rest of the day.

"Do you think that you have enough to work on for the next two or three days?" Jake asked.

Josh was finishing up for the day, "Yeah, I think so," he replied. "If not, there is always something to work on around this place."

Jake smiled. "You've got that right." After helping Josh with the cleanup, Jake headed home.

The next day was a hot May day. Brenda had invited her friends over for a dip in the pool. When Josh got to the wood-pile, he took his shirt off and placed it on a log nearby and went to work. Brenda and the girls had been diving into the pool for sometimes now so when Brenda climbed up on the diving board this time, her friend, David noticed that Brenda would occasionally look over in Josh's direction. He was annoyed and asked her. "Why do you keep looking at him?"

Brenda's friend Grace chimed in. "Because he's a good-looker," she said.

David was angry. "I thought you were told not to talk to him anymore."

Brenda grew steadily more upset at David's possessiveness. She thought of those words as an effort to try to enforce the words of her grandmother. She swam to the other side of the pool, crawled up on the deck, and sat into her lawn chair.

Seeing Brenda's irritation, Grace left the pool as well. She walked over to where Brenda was sitting and said, "Pay no attention to David. He's just running off at the mouth." Grace pulled a chair over beside her friend and tried to sooth her anger.

"I'm getting a bit sick of him trying to run my life," Brenda said.

Grace leaned over and whispered, "I was looking at him too." She giggled.

"I know that you were." Then they shared a silent moment while Brenda whispered, "You're just sneakier than me." After their laugh, Grace became serious.

"Don't say anything. If my folks found out that I was taking a peek at a black man, my butt would be mud."

Brenda shook her head in agreement. "Don't worry. Your secret is safe with me." Now that she was relaxed, her anger faded. She went back to the pool but this time dove in from the side.

The next morning, Josh was stacking the freshly cut wood on the back porch when Brenda came into the kitchen. She watched him for a minute before speaking.

"Hello, Josh," Brenda was pleasant. "How are you doing today?"

Josh looked at Brenda coldly. "I'm fine." After stacking the wood neatly, he turned and walked away. Brenda was upset that he said nothing. He had acted as if she was not even there. *The nerve of him,* she thought. He works for my father and won't even speak casually to me. She was exceedingly upset when she left the kitchen.

The following day, Brenda was sitting on the front porch of her grandparents' house reading a novel. She heard a low rumble and something caught her eye, off to her right, she noticed a cloud of dust at the far end of the road. The cloud of dust followed a car to the front of the house where she was sitting. David had just brought a new car and was rushing over to show it to Brenda. When the car stopped, she left her book and went to see it up close.

"Let's go for a ride," said David excitedly. Brenda hopped into the car and off they went east of her house and down a path that led over to Swamp Town, then down to the creek. After he pulled over, Brenda jumped out, walked over to the knoll, and lay down in the tall grass that overlooked the creek. Absentmindedly, she said, "This is a beautiful spot."

David looked at Brenda fondly. "Yeah, I like it here," he replied. It was a warm day with a soft wind blowing from the east. The Spanish moss waved from the cypress trees as if to welcome them, and the water rippled from an occasional dip in the creek by a frog who needed to cool off. It was a lazy day and the whole world seemed to be at ease. David walked over to where Brenda lay among the grass and flowers that were scattered over the entire knoll. Sitting beside her, he wanted to know more about her feelings.

"How do you like this beautiful place? David asked, feeling the cool breeze as he brushed his hair away from his eyes.

"It's great out here," Brenda said. "I've walked out here many times."

"With Grace?" he asked, looking at her softly.

Brenda was in her own world. "No. I walked mostly alone." Brenda was relaxed now so David decided not to ask any further questions. He placed his arms around her shoulders, looked deep into her blue-green eyes, and kissed her on her soft lips. Feeling the cool breeze, they watched the evening sun sink slowly below the horizon.

After that evening with Brenda, David was sure that she was his girl. He decided to drop by the next evening uninvited. She saw him walking up the walkway, so she walked out on the porch and sat on the swing.

Brenda was surprised to see him. So before he sat down, she said, "I'm not swimming today."

"That's all right," David replied. "I'm here to talk with you."

She motioned him to sit down. "What is it?"

Suddenly, David was nervous. He could feel that her attitude of today was completely different than that of yesterday. He coughed before asking, "Are you planning to live in this area after you graduate from high school?"

"Why do you ask?" She looked up the road not really paying much attention to him.

"I just wanted to know if I would be able to see you when I wanted to."

Brenda hid a small laugh. "I'm not planning that far ahead," she said. "I may go to the coast and spend some time with my grandfather. He's a fisherman, you know."

David did not like how the conversation was headed. "I don't like fishing," David said. "I was thinking that we could live around here."

Brenda was not sure of what David wanted. "I'm not thinking about settling down. I'm going to do some traveling."

David became more unsure of himself. "But I thought that we were going to be together." His voice was now quieter when he said those words.

Brenda stifled another laugh. "You are a little bit too controlling for me." David was now shocked. He said nothing as he got up from the swing and walked away. Brenda just sat there swaying backward and forward in the porch swing.

The next day, Brenda had invited Grace over for a swim. They were sitting in the shallow end of the pool when Grace asked her what had happened between her and David.

Brenda told her, "We went up on the knoll the other night." Brenda really wanted to tell her friend the truth but hesitated.

"What did you do?"

"You know, we were playing around."

Grace couldn't help but laugh. "Brenda, you mean, you made out, don't you?"

Brenda hesitated. "Well, you know what I mean."

"Yeah, I know." Grace could see that Brenda was anxious.

"Well, now he's talking like I'm his for keeps," Brenda said with a worried look on her face.

"Did he ask you to marry him?"

Looking off into the distance and thinking that she didn't want to get married to him or anyone else, Brenda finally realized why she didn't want David. "I didn't give him a chance. I don't want to marry anyone." She was mostly thinking to herself.

Grace thought otherwise and asked, "Are you sure that that's the only reason?"

Still in her world, she replied, "What do you mean, Grace?

Grace knew that Brenda's heart was with someone else and she knew who it was.

"You know," she said.

Looking way off in the far distance, Brenda didn't realize how transparent she was. "Are you crazy?" She couldn't look Grace in the eyes. "You know that I can't have a thing for Josh." She looked away again. "He's black you know."

"Yeah, I know it and you know it, but if you moved up north, who would know it?" Grace could now see how deep Brenda's feelings for Josh really was.

Brenda leaned back into the water and gently pushed herself away from the edge of the pool and swam away toward the deep end of the pool with a slow backstroke.

Watching her, Grace knew that she was thinking of what had been said. Suddenly, Grace was having mixed emotions. *What if she really left this area? How would I get to see my best friend?* All kinds of thoughts flooded her mind. Brenda was nearly at the other end of the pool when Grace pushed herself away from the edge of the pool and swam toward her. Not to catch her, just to be near her friend. It was like a very slow race that no one wanted to win. By the time that Grace got back to the shallow end of the pool, Brenda was out of the water and drying herself off.

"I'm going into the house. Stay as long as you like." She walked away, deep in thought.

Brenda went to her house and up to her room. She lay there, thinking of her future. She had another year of high school so there was no real reason to rush anything, but there were lots of things on her mind and none of them had marriage in them. There was one thing that she did know and that was she could not find David in any of her plans.

It was late in the evening when Mr. Williams and his wife got home. Mr. Williams walked around the property, checking to see how well Josh had done the work that he had been hired to do. When he got to the rear of the house, Josh was stacking the last of the wood that he had split in a pile so that it could be dried out. As usual, Mr. Williams was pleased with the young man's work. "I see that you have a pretty good amount of wood in the drying pile and the yard is looking very good."

"Thank you, sir." Josh replied. "Sam came over and gave me a hand."

"How much work did he do?" Mr. Williams asked.

"He was here two full days, helping with the large logs."

"Good. When you are finish out here, come to the house and I'll give you your money and a check for Jake."

"Yes, sir."

Marge had gone into the house and walked into the kitchen. She asked Sarah for a cold drink.

"Coming right up," Sarah said. "Would you like lemonade?"

"That will be just fine," Marge replied. "By the way, have you seen Brenda lately?"

"She went up to her room about an hour ago."

Marge sat down in a chair at the kitchen table and took a sip of her lemonade, which had a pink color.

"This is good, Sarah. What's that pink coloring in it?" Marge asked.

"Oh just a bit of cherry Kool-Aid."

Marge took another sip and headed upstairs to speak to Brenda after thanking Sarah for the drink. As Marge climbed the stairway, she called for her daughter. "Brenda! Brenda, you up there? What are you doing, honey?"

Brenda didn't really feel like talking to her mother but answered anyway. "Just resting, Mom. Come on up." She sighed.

At the top of the stairs, Marge saw her daughter lying on her bed. "Where have you and Dad been?" Brenda asked.

"We went over to the east side of the property, checking the crops and talking to the tenants. You know that father of yours, he wants to take care of the property like his father asked him to do. How did your day go?"

"Not too bad," Brenda said with a blank look on her face.

Marge could always tell when her daughter was upset. "What's wrong now? Did you and David break up?"

"Yes," Brenda said with no emotion.

"Why?" Marge asked.

Brenda sighed again. "He started getting too serious. He was asking me what I was going to do after finishing school, suggesting that we stay here and getting into my business. When I told him that I was thinking of maybe moving to Baton Rouge, he got very angry and left."

Marge was not angry at her daughter. "I don't think that you are old enough to be thinking about that kind of stuff. I want you to finish high school and go on to college."

Relieved, Brenda relaxed. "Then you are not upset that we have broken up?"

"Not at all, you are too young to be thinking about such things. For now, I just want you to concentrate on finishing high school."

As the two continued their conversation, Mr. Williams passed his daughter's room; he saw his wife and daughter talking and wanted to be sure that all was well. "What are you two girls talking about?" Mr. Williams was amused, seeing them so serious.

"Oh, nothing," Marge said, "just planning our future."

"Just make sure that I'm in it," he called from his bedroom door. "By the way, Brenda, when you and your mother are finish, come and get these checks and take them down to Josh."

A few moments later, she went into her parents' room and saw the check on the dresser. Her mind raced. She wasn't even listening to her father.

"The checks are right there on the desk. Give them both to Josh," her father said.

Brenda didn't hear a word. She picked the checks up off the desk and left the room. "Now Josh will have to say something to me," she said to herself.

When Brenda came down the stairs, she went out the kitchen door, looking around for Josh. Josh had just completed his work and was now sitting on a log near the woodpile, putting his shirt back on.

Brenda couldn't understand why she was so nervous. She walked over close to him and said, "Hi, Josh. You through working for the day?"

The young man was not moved. "Yes," Josh replied.

"I have something for you," Brenda said, trying to control her nerves.

Josh stood up, his shirt hanging off one shoulder. "What is it?"

With her nerves calmed, she decided to go for it. She ignored his question and continued speaking. "Did you ever notice me looking at you from the pool?"

"I thought you were checking to see how much wood that I had cut."

She paid no attention to his answer. "I was looking at your broad shoulders and those abs of yours," she said boldly.

Josh did not wish too seem impressive but his nature caused him to straighten up, exposing his entire torso. "I thought you were told not to talk to me." His words slapped Brenda cold. She was now really upset.

"I'll talk to whoever I wish! Here is your check." She turned and walked away. She was angry at what he had said to her, yet she desired him even more.

Josh went to the Williams's kitchen and told his mother that he was going to the creek and do a little fishing. Since his friend Jack left, Josh did most of his fishing alone. Today, Josh had to deliver a check to Alice's father so he went by his house, picked up his fishing gear, and walked over to give Jake his check. Jake saw him coming and met him at the door.

"Mr. Williams asked me to bring you your check," he said to Mr. Wilson.

"Thanks a lot," Jake told him, "I sure can use it."

Josh could hear stirring in the backroom. "Is that you, Josh?" Alice called out from the back.

"Yeah, it's me." Josh replied.

Alice was happy to see him. "You going fishing?" Alice asked, wanting to go.

Josh said yes and asked her to join him.

Alice came to the door, wearing blue jeans, cut-off shorts with a red long-sleeved blouse, tied in a knot just above the navel and worn-out tennis shoes—worn only to protect the soles of her feet. They walked down to the stable to the place where Bert used to keep his fishing gear. She picked out a rod and reel and some hooks then she asked Josh if he had enough bait for the both of them.

"We have plenty of bait," Josh replied.

The two of them walked back up to the path and down to Jesse's place. From there, they went down to the area of the creek where the water was much deeper. When they got to Josh's favorite spot, Josh mentioned that this is where they keep the big boys—referring to the catfish.

It had been sometime since someone had placed a large log about four feet from the edge of the creek and parallel to the water. It is unknown how many people had sat there over the years, but today, this seat belonged to Josh and Alice.

Before Josh could get his gear together, Alice was in his bait bucket of worms, preparing to bait her hook. After baiting her hook, she stood up and cast her line to the edge of a bed of large water lilies. As the bait settled to the bottom, Alice walked back over to the log, sat down and said, "That's where the big boys are." Alice had cast into Josh's favorite spot.

He threw his line into his second best spot. They sat there for five minutes or so but there were no nibbles, not even the movement of frogs or turtles moving about. Then all of a sudden, there was a tug on Josh's line. Jumping to his feet, Josh got cocky. "Let me show you how to catch a fish!" he shouted. He grinned while snatching his line and started to reel in the fish. "Now we'll see who can do some real fishing. I can smell him frying now."

Alice enjoyed watching him get so excited. "That's a nice one," she said. "But I'm going to get the big boy."

While they fished for an hour or so, Josh caught a couple of sunfish and one small cat. Alice had caught nothing. She reeled in her line and cast out again. This time, she cast to the opposite end of the lily pads, letting it sink down to the bottom. Then she gave it a little jiggle and tightened the line. Josh was watching her every move. She sat back down with her hand on the reel and the tip of one finger on the line. She was looking straight ahead. Josh could see her twitch every now and then. All of a sudden, he saw her jump to her feet and said, "I got you now." She tightened up on her line, then stepped across the log so that she could give the fish room to move around and wear himself out. She followed the fish thirty feet down the bank of the creek, reeling in the line just enough to draw him in closer and closer. When she realized that the fish was tired out, she called to Josh. "Get the net!" She laughed. "I've got the big boy!"

Josh came over with the net and helped her pull in a fifteen-pound catfish.

It was a good day of fishing. Josh liked being with Alice. He was very happy that he had asked her to be his girlfriend. They sat there until nearly dark, talking about the things they liked and what they wanted to do in life. Josh got up from his seat on the log, walked over to the edge of the water. When he returned, he sat down close to her.

She smiled knowing that he could have sat close to her by just moving over two feet but she liked his move. He placed his arms around her shoulders and she leaned in closer…they kissed.

On their way back home, they stopped at Jesse Mae's place. Josh wanted to go in and get a drink. When they walked in, Jessie who was behind the bar said. "Hello, young folks, you been fishing?"

"Yeah," Josh said. "I caught a few."

Alice nudged him. "I caught the biggest one."

Jesse teased Josh. "You let her catch the biggest one?" she said while smiling as she held up one of his smaller fish.

"I didn't let her," Josh said. "She is a better fisherperson than I am."

"Jessie laughed out loud when she heard the phase 'better fisherperson.' That sounded good," she said and repeated it. "Fisherperson."

"I'll have a Dr. Pepper," Alice said, changing the subject.

"Me too," Josh added. They had a nice relaxing break, enjoying their cold drink and chatting with Jesse Mae.

On their way home, the two of them stopped at Alice's house and cleaned the fish. They shared the big catfish and by the time Sarah got home, Josh had fried fresh fish for his mother who had spent the entire day cooking for someone else. Sarah entered the house smelling the aroma.

"I smell fish, my boy is cooking his mother some fresh caught catfish?" she said and sat at the table where she was served by Josh, just as she had served the Williamses. It was a good feeling and she felt so blessed that her son was thinking of her. That night before she slept, she smiled and cried a bit, knowing that her boy was becoming a man.

CHAPTER 9

IT WAS GETTING close to graduation and Josh was constantly thinking of what he was going to do when school was over. One day after school that following week, Josh asked Mr. Smith if he could speak with him.

"Of course, you can," Mr. Smith told him. "Just remain after school and we will talk." After school was over for the day, Josh and Mr. Smith had their talk.

"What's on your mind?" Mr. Smith asked.

"I'm trying to think of what I'm going to do after graduation," Josh said.

"What do you want to do?"

"I thought of going over to Tuskegee to see if I could get registered in school there."

"Why don't you give it a try? I think that you will have a very good chance of getting in school there."

"Do you really think that I can do that?"

The teacher smiled. "Of course you can and I'll help you."

That afternoon, Mr. Smith gave Josh all the information that he needed to get into Tuskegee. He also told Josh that he would tutor him in all the things that he needed to know to pass the entrance exams.

"What about money?" Josh asked.

"They have a work program there, I'm sure that I can help you get a job."

Josh was exceedingly happy. He had no idea that he had a chance of getting into college. He ran all the way home to tell his mother what Mr. Smith had told him. When Sarah got home that evening, Josh was waiting at the door. Before she entered the house, Josh excitedly greeted her at the door, saying, "Guess what! Guess what!" All the time grinning happily. Sarah could see that her son was about to burst. "I'm going to school…I'm going to school!" He said, picking her up in his arms.

Sarah could see the joy. "I know you are going to school," she said. "You will be graduating next week."

"No! No! Mom," he exclaimed. "I mean, I'll be going to college. I'm going to Tuskegee." Sarah couldn't say anything. She hugged him tightly while the tears ran down from her eyes.

The next morning, Sarah was filled with joy when she went to work. On her way to the kitchen, she kept saying to herself, "Josh is going to school…Josh is going to school." The smile on her face was huge and there was a pep in her step. She felt so good that she decided to make everyone their favorite breakfast.

The smell of the family's favorite food awakened them and one by one they came through the kitchen door with a smile on their faces. Grandma Williams, who knew Sarah best, asked her. "What's up, Sarah? You have such a radiant look on your face."

Sarah could not hold her news any longer. She just had to let it out. "Josh is going to college!" She exclaimed. "My boy is going to college." When they heard the news, everyone had a smile on their faces except Brenda. She took a couple of bites of her food, then silently left the table. As the rest of the family congratulated Sarah for Josh's good news and continued to enjoy their special food, Brenda had gotten dressed and was on her way to her friend Grace's house.

It was nearly nine o'clock that morning when she approached Grace's driveway. Grace's father was just leaving for work at the bank in Baton Rouge. He waved at Brenda as she entered the lane leading to his house, wondering why she was up so early. Brenda saw Grace sitting in the swing on the porch. She walked up and sat down beside her without saying a word.

"What going on?" Grace asked while slowly, swaying back and forth in the swing.

Brenda was pouting. "Nothing," she mumbled.

Grace swayed gently. "What do you mean nothing? You are up walking in the road at eight o'clock in the morning and you say nothing is going on? Don't tell me nothing is happening. I'm your best friend, remember."

"Well I did have a good breakfast this morning," Brenda said, as she sat heavily on the swing beside Grace.

"That can't be it. There has to be something else, so go ahead and tell me." Grace insisted.

Brenda was angry. "That Sarah, all happy and full of cheer, came in this morning and cooked us our favorite breakfast and then. Guess what she said?"

Grace stopped swaying. "What?"

Brenda sighed. "She said that Josh was going to college."

Grace rolled her eyes. "So, what's your problem?" She went back to her swaying.

"If he goes to college, he won't be here," Brenda said.

"Are you saying that you are in love with him and don't want him to leave?" Grace asked. "Have you been talking to him?"

"I tried a couple of times, but he won't talk back."

Grace looked at her friend, confused. "I don't get it," she said. "You were told not to talk to him. He won't talk to you and you don't want him to leave. I just don't get it." Grace shook her head. "What college is he going to?"

Brenda sat on the swing. "He's going to some black school in Alabama. Why didn't he go to school with us?"

Grace looked at Brenda with amazement. "You know why he didn't go to school with us, he's black, and you know that."

"His skin is as light as mine."

"I know, but his mother is black."

Thinking out loud, Brenda said, "What if we went up north, do you think that we could be together up there?"

Grace gave her friend a long look. "You are getting ahead of yourself, Brenda. You don't even know if he wants to be with you."

Brenda stood up, wiped a tear from her eye, and walked away. Grace was confused, wondering what was on Brenda's mind. She knew that Brenda liked his looks, but could not believe that she could be in love with him. She watched as Brenda walked all the way back to her house. Once home, Brenda went to her room. Her mother had watched her daughter leave and was waiting for her. She quietly knocked on the door, "Brenda," she said. "I thought I saw you going outside."

Brenda let her in, not really wanting to talk. "You did," Brenda said. They both sat on the bed.

"What's up?" Marge asked.

"Nothing. I just wanted to talk to Grace." Marge could see the sadness in her eyes.

"Come on, I'm your mother. You can talk to me about anything." She pressed on. "Is it David?"

Brenda could not look at her mom. "It's not David. I was just wondering how Josh is going to be able to go to college."

"Is that all? His teacher is going to help him. He will be in that black school in Alabama. You should be happy for him."

Frustrated, Brenda threw her head on her pillow. "Well, I'm not...I'm not happy at all."

Marge rubbed her child's back, not truly knowing what was going on. "You are just a little jealous about him going to school. Honey, you will be able to go to school, too. You will be able to pick any school in the country. I'll make sure of that."

Brenda closed her eyes. No one understood what her problem was and she didn't dare tell her mother the real truth.

That evening, Josh went by Alice's house and asked her if she would like to go for a walk down to Jesse Mae's place. "Sure," she said, hugging him. "You going to buy me a soda?"

Josh hugged her back. "Of course, I'll buy you anything." He paused then said, "Up to fifty cents, that is."

They shared a laugh. "I'll settle for a soda," Alice said. As they walked toward Jesse Mae's place, Josh told her about his chance of going to school. Alice was very happy for him. "I wish I could go to school," Alice was sad thinking of losing him.

"Who knows"—Josh had other plans—"If we stay together and I finish school, I can send you to school."

Alice was surprised. "Do you mean if we get married, Josh?" She smiled, taking this all in.

"Of course I do, Alice. When I finish college, I'll be able to take care of you." Josh moved to one side of the road, taking Alice's hand making sure that she would be out of the way of an oncoming car. As the car passed them, he could see that the passengers in the car were Brenda's friend Grace and her boyfriend, but he thought nothing of it at the time.

The two of them continued their walk to Jesse Mae's place. When they got there, no one was in sight and then a familiar voice called out from the back.

"You kids have a seat," the voice said. "I'll be right there."

Josh and Alice went over to a table and had a seat. A few minutes later, Jesse Mae came over with two grape sodas and had a seat with the youngsters. Jesse Mae and the young couple laughed and talked for about an hour and a half.

Jesse Mae told stories about her time up north. She told about how she had been in love with Bert and what a good man he was, but when she thought of his death, the tears came to her eyes and the sorrow invaded her heart, so she got up and walked behind the counter for a towel to wipe the tears away. Taking to heart her sadness, the couple decided to walk over to say their good-byes.

Alice walked over to where Jesse Mae was standing and said, "I'll see you later, Miss Jesse Mae." She touched her hand to let Miss Jesse Mae know that she felt her pain. On their way back, they spoke very little to each other. They knew that something was wrong with Miss Jesse Mae, but they had no idea what it was. Josh walked Alice to the porch, squeezed her hand gently, and told her that he would see her later.

When Josh got home, he saw Grace drove away from the front of Brenda's house. He thought nothing of it, so he sat in a chair on his front porch for a relaxing rest in the cool of the evening.

Monday was the beginning of the last week of school for Josh. He had had his last conference with Mr. Smith concerning his entrance to Tuskegee and had found out that he had been approved. He walked home alone needing to have the time to let it all sink in. When he got to his house, he walked around to his animals that he had kept since he was six years old. *I'll ask Mama to give them away as they were given to me*, he thought, looking at them with pride. He walked out onto the porch but it did not relax him, so he got his fishing gear and headed down to the fishing hole. He cast his line in the water without bait and sat down with his head resting on a small branch. He closed his eyes and tried to imagine all the things that had happened to him. *Life was good*, he thought as he dozed off to sleep.

Josh liked to be alone—he wanted to be alone. He could feel himself as he drifted away. He had been sleeping for a half hour or so when from a distance, he heard a twig snap. He wasn't sure of what it was. He heard something, but it did not fully awaken him. Then he heard another snap. This sound fully awakened him. Still groggy, he looked around and there standing not more than fifteen feet from where he lay was Brenda. She had watched him sleep.

"Hello, Josh," she said. "Can I fish with you?"

"I'm getting ready to leave," he said, hoping that she would take the hint. Josh started to gather his gear.

"You can't leave now. We have some talking to do!" Brenda said as she sat down, her bare legs nearly touching his. "You can't run now. There is no one here to hear us." She moved over close to him and took hold of his arm.

Josh kept getting his things together with his other arm. "Please leave," he begged her quietly. "Are you trying to get me killed?"

Brenda held on. "I just want to talk, and if you leave now, I'll tell everyone that you brought me out here and left me."

Josh stood up and walked over to the log by the bank of the creek. He sat down, thinking he must not make her angry. He must calm her down. "I didn't bring you out here," he said, trying to control his temper.

"You brought that Alice out here!" Brenda shouted.

Josh could see that she was getting upset and tried a bit harder to calm her down. "She just came out here with me to do a little fishing," said Josh calmly.

Brenda was wearing short shorts and the top of a two-piece swimsuit. She sat down beside him with her legs touching his, and she put her arms around his shoulder. "Come on," she said. "Be nice to me." She was speaking calmly now and this scared Josh the most.

Josh, in his nervousness, stood up, thinking, *I can't let this happen. What if someone sees me. If the Klan catches me, I'm a dead man.* Sweat started to foam on his forehead. He was afraid. There was no way to win. If he did what she wanted, he could get hung. If he didn't do it, he could get hung.

She slowly slid down to the ground beside the log, taking his hand and pulled him down with her. Her caresses were causing all of his resistance and most of his fears to fade. The boldness of her actions overwhelmed all of the things that his mother had ever taught him. His head was telling him no, but his body just let it happen.

When it was over, Brenda got up, dressed herself, and walked away without saying a word. She walked through the cornfield to the road that passed Grace's house and went into the dressing room of the swimming pool. She stripped down to the buff and dived into the pool. It was as if she was trying to cleanse herself off the dirty deed that she had done. She swam ten laps before quitting. Then she wrapped herself in a towel and ran up to her room.

Josh was sitting on the log as if nothing had happened. He hoped that she would not tell anyone and thought no one had seen them—that is, until he looked across the creek and saw a fisherman with a full view of the area in which he stood. It was clear that the man had a view of everything, but he must have thought that Josh was white because of his light skin color. Josh decided that he had better leave in a hurry before the man figured out who he really was. He calmed himself and walked as normal as he could. With his fishing gear in his hands, he made his way to Jesse Mae's place.

Looking at the fishing gear, Jesse asked. "Where is the fish?" Josh was still on edge. "Didn't get any today, but I'll get them the next time."

"Are you ready for school?"

He was anxious. "I can't wait to get away from here," he said. He was hoping to get out of town before the news got out about what had happened down at the creek. It was very hot and he was sweating for more reasons than one and needed to get home and relax.

Josh walked slowly toward his house, trying to think of what to do even though he didn't initiate the action down by the creek. He would be off to college in a few days and he was hoping that Brenda would just keep her mouth shut. When he got home, he had a seat on the front porch where he could see or hear if there was any excitement going on at the Williams's house. He heard none so he relaxed there for the rest of the evening.

Brenda had relaxed herself in the pool and no one had seen her enter the house so she was satisfied that no one had witnessed any of her actions. She made plans that evening to ask Marge if she could go to visit her grandfather on the Gulf Coast for the summer.

Josh worked very hard for the next few days chopping wood, cleaning the yard and pool. He wanted to collect all the money that he could get for school.

Brenda got her permission to visit her grandfather for the summer. She enjoyed the first days with her grandfather, but after a few days of working on the shrimp boat, the physical work had worn her out and she longed for those days of relaxing with her friends at the pool, but she wouldn't give up. She had begged for permission to visit her grandfather so she would have to stick it out.

Josh was to leave for college the week that Brenda returned from her visit to New Orleans. As soon as she got to the house, she went to the kitchen where she knew his mother would be. "Did Josh leave for school yet?" Brenda asked, trying to make herself seem nonchalant.

"Not yet," Sarah replied. "He'll be leaving in a day or so."

"I'm glad he got into school," Brenda replied. "Is mom here?" She was fidgeting and Sarah could see it.

"No," Sarah said. "She and your father went to Baton Rouge this morning. They should be back in an hour or so."

"I'll be upstairs, let me know when they get home, will you, Sarah?"

Sarah watched Brenda carefully. "Your grandmother is out in the garden, did you see her when you came in?" Sarah asked.

"No, I'll go out and find her. Brenda's acting was a little odd. Sarah thought, *Why didn't she ask about her grandmother when she came in?* She shook it off and went back to work. Brenda went out to the garden and spoke to her grandmother but left without saying how she had enjoyed her visit with her grandfather. She went up to her bedroom and laid down to rest until her parents came home.

Grace, who had seen Brenda get out of the car when she arrived at her house, decided to come over for a visit. Sarah, hearing the knock on the front door, answered it and welcomed Grace in. She went to the bottom of the stairs and called for Brenda. "Brenda, Grace is here to see you."

Brenda replied that she was coming downstairs. She put on some fresh clothes and rushed down to see her friend. They hugged for a while, having really missed each other. "Let's go out to the pool and relax. I've got something to tell you," she whispered.

"I was hoping you would say that. I've got my swimsuit on under my clothes." The two of them ran out to the pool, stripping their outer clothes as they went along. They dived in, swimming a couple of laps to cool off. Then they climbed out of the pool and sat in the lounge chairs to relax.

Drying herself off, Grace looked at Brenda with anticipation. "Now what was that you had to tell me?"

"I don't know if I should tell you this," Brenda said softly.

"Why not?" Grace asked. "I'm your best friend, you can tell me anything."

"Maybe I should tell my mom first."

Grace was quick. "Ooh! My goodness, you're pregnant."

Brenda was shocked. "How did you come to that conclusion?"

"There is only one thing that you have to tell your mother before you tell your best friend and that is that you are pregnant." Grace wanted the juice. "Who is the father? Is it David? It's David!" she shouted.

Brenda asked her to be quiet. "Shut up," Brenda said. "I'm not going to tell you anything else. And you had better not tell anyone until I tell my mom." It was then that Brenda decided that she had better go ahead and tell her mother and get it over with.

Grace could see that her friend was nervous. She was trembling and a tear formed in her eyes so Grace stayed with her, helping her to get her clothes on and walking with her to the door. Then she left and went home. She was truly concerned for her friend and wished her well.

After checking the crops on the west side of Swamp Town, Mr. Williams and Marge had gone to Baton Rouge to do a little shopping.

Marge had asked him, "Are you taking me to dinner?"

"Why do you ask?" he replied.

"Because you're so handsome."

"We are going to the big town. We might as well have a good time," he told her. "By the way, is Brenda supposed to come home tonight?"

"Yes," said Marge. She should be home when we get back.

While we are out, I thought that I would stop by the bank and talk to the banker about the price of that new Ford tractor that just came out. I'm told that it's very handy. After that, I'm yours for the rest of the day.

"Speaking of Brenda," Marge said. "I think there is something going on with her that she is not telling me."

"Like what?" Robert asked. "What could she be doing down there on the Gulf Coast." Let's give her a little time, it may be nothing. Meanwhile, let's enjoy the evening."

As soon as they got to Baton Rouge, Robert went to the manager's desk at the bank to talk business about a tractor that he had planned to buy. Marge went to a cashier to withdraw some money to buy some of the things that she had in mind. After acquiring the funds that she wanted, she went over to the lounge area to wait for her husband. When Robert showed up at the lounge, Marge asked him why he had to go to the bank manager to talk about buying a tractor.

"Because he has one of those new Ford tractors," he said and I wanted to ask him how efficient the machine was and how much it cost. Besides, I like to talk to him and you never know when you might need a banker. "Where are we going to have lunch?"

"Why don't we go to Betty Jo's place? They say they serve some great shrimp there." Marge suggested.

"That sound just fine to me."

At lunch, Robert asked, "Do you think that Brenda is pregnant?"

"Where did that come from?"

"Oh! I don't know. I was just thinking about what you said, you know. That bit about something being wrong."

They went into Betty Jo's place. This was a fancy restaurant, one with fine decorations and a reputation of having the best food in town and Robert Jr. was known well enough to be seated by the owner at Betty Jo's place.

Marge had the shrimp platter, while Robert had the crab cake platter. It was a lovely lunch filled with light talk and laughter, then it was time for Marge to do some shopping. To Robert's surprise, most of what she bought was for him. She bought him three suits—one black, one brown, and one blue. Then she had him carry his suits to the shoe department where she bought him two pairs of shoes. With these items in his arms, he followed her to the shirts department where she purchased six matching shirts along with a supply of underclothes. Robert had no idea that he needed so much to wear or that his wife had been keeping up with it.

When they got back to the house, Brenda's father dropped Marge off at the house and headed back off to the barbershop. Marge came into the house with an arm full of things that she had purchased in Baton Rouge.

Mrs. Williams was in the living room reading. "How did it go today?" Mrs. Williams asked.

"Just fine," Marge replied. "Just let me get these things upstairs and I'll be back downstairs to talk with you." She went upstairs and put her things into her bedroom. When she walked back out her door, Brenda was standing in her doorway.

"I've got something to tell you," she said.

Marge could plainly see the concern on her child's face. Brenda took her mother to her room and sat down at the foot of her bed.

"What's on your mind, honey? Did you have a good time at Grandpa's house?"

Brenda could not stop the fidgeting. "Yes, I had a good time at Grandpa's place, but he worked the crap out of me."

"So what's bothering my little girl?" Marge asked, looking into her eyes for clues, trying to pick up on what was going on.

Brenda just said it without hesitation, "I think I'm pregnant."

Marge closed her eyes and fell back across the foot of Brenda's bed.

Brenda looked at her mother and saw a tear form in the corners of both of her eyes. She had never felt such pain as that which she felt when she saw the tears in her mother's eyes.

Marge reached out and took a corner of the sheet of the bed and wiped her eyes. "So you went to Grandpa's house and went wild?" Marge's voice started to rise. "What were you thinking?" Trying to keep her voice under control and wiping the tears from her eyes.

Brenda said nothing. She did not want to add a lie by saying that it happened on her visit with Grandpa. The pain was more than Brenda could bear. She fell to her knees with her face in her mother's lap; her tears soaked her mother's clothes.

Her mother wrapped her arms around her daughter's shoulders. She soothed her and said, "We'll get through this, your mom will take care of you. Your mother will make everything all right."

"Brenda was not finished. "There is more, Mama, I've got to tell you everything." She walked to a chair on the other side of the room and sat down with her head in her hands. She told the whole story about meeting Josh at the creek and what she did.

"It was about a week before school closed and Grace stopped by and told me that she had seen Josh and that girl Alice walking down to Jesse Mae's place together. She said that they were holding hands. The next time I saw Josh, he was going to the fishing hole. I followed him. I thought that she was going to meet him down there but she was not there. I approached him. At first, he said no, he didn't want me. I told him that if he didn't do it, I would tell everyone that he forced me. He tried to walk away, but I insisted. Now I'm pregnant."

There was an uncomfortable silence. Mrs. Williams could hear Marge and her daughter upstairs sobbing. The sound drew her and Sarah, who was standing in the kitchen door, to the foot of the steps. They both knew that something was seriously wrong and Mrs. Williams had an idea what it was.

The doorknob turned on the front door. It was Mr. Williams. He strolled in with a smile on his face. He had had a good day and was ready for a shower or maybe going for a dip in the pool. He did not often get much of a chance of taking a dip in the pool since there was always youngsters there, but the pool was empty today, and Mr. Williams was ready to relax for the rest of the day.

When he walked through the doorway, he saw his mother with a concerned look on her face. The relaxation was over. "What's up?" he asked his mother.

Mrs. Williams was sitting in a chair by the front window. "Your wife and your daughter are having some problems."

His mother's words worried him. "What the hell," said Mr. Williams, as he rushed up the stairs to see what was going on.

His family was clutched on the bed, eyes red from tears. Quietly, his wife told her husband what her daughter had told her. After a few minutes of silence, the three of them walked slowly downstairs. Mr. Williams was heard to say, "That black SOB." His anger was thick and wicked. "I'll kill him!" he shouted.

.Sarah turned and walked back to the kitchen and placed her head on the table. The tears came and did not stop. Mrs. Williams stood to her feet, angry at her son. "You will do no such thing, Junior," she told him. "You are the cause of all of this. You are the one who has brought shame to this family. Not Josh or Brenda."

Marge was confused. "What in God's name is this all about?" she cried. "It cannot just be that she is pregnant. There has to be more to this."

Mrs. Williams said to her son. "You don't really know what is going on here, do you?" She was disgusted. "Have you lost your memory?"

"What do you mean, Ma?"

"Have you forgotten what happened in that kitchen nineteen years ago?"

Junior had a blank look on his face but inside his head, a storm of memories formed. In the center of the storm, he could see himself committing a hideous act that he had forced to the back of his mind. He saw himself forcing Sarah to the floor of the kitchen. He heard the screams and saw the tears he had caused. When he realized that his mother was still talking, he heard her say, "Don't you remember seeing yourself, the thing that you did to Sarah? Can't you see that Josh is the product of your action? Have you not noticed that Josh and Brenda are brother and sister?"

Junior finally understood. "I didn't know... I swear, I didn't know."

"Well, he is yours," his mother said, "and I am as much to blame as you are." That they didn't know that they are siblings. The old woman shook her head. "The lies were out now for all to see. The secrets that were kept, them not knowing that they are sister and brother."

Mrs. Williams sat back down in the chair. The memories came back like a storm. Tears began running down her cheeks. "I was in the house," she said. "I saw you when you ran out after raping her. I begged Sarah to keep it a secret and promised her that I would help take care of my grandson, your child. I love Josh. He is my flesh and blood." With finality, she said, "And he is your son, Brenda's brother!"

Marge was shocked. It took some time for her to get herself together. Her words would not form into sentences. After a few moments, Marge whispered, "My husband is a rapist and my grandchild will be the child of my daughter and my husband's son." There were no more tears for her. Without looking at her man, she walked out of the house.

After the revelation, Sarah felt a bit relieved but she could not trust the Williamses. She had to protect her son. She got up from the table and said, "I'm going home." She had to warn Josh, no matter what pain Junior had caused her and whatever the truth revealed. She had to get him out of town. *If the KKK found out about this*, she thought, *he might as well be dead*. When she got to the house, she was nearly running. Out of breath, and she was frantic, shaking all over.

"Josh! Josh!" she called. Sarah ran through each room yelling. "Where are you?" Josh had been in the back when he heard the commotion. He rushed to the door to see what his mother was concerned about.

Sarah was breathing heavily. "They are over there talking about you, Josh."

Josh had no clue. He thought that things had settled down. He thought that if she hadn't told anyone by now, it would be all over. "About me?" Josh asked.

"Yes, you and that Brenda." She could hardly get her breath. "They know what you did," she said, starting to look for his clothes. "I want you to get away from here and do it now!"

Josh finally understood. Ashamed, he tried to explain. "But Ma, she approached me. I told her that I did not want to do it. Then she said that if I did not do it, she would say that I forced her."

Sarah looked at her son. Their anger and my sadness, it's all the same. "No one is going to believe you, Josh. Go to your friends at that school, maybe they can help you."

Josh quickly grabbed a few things from his room. He took Bert's .45 that had been given to Bert by Mr. Williams. He left home going in the direction of the bus stop, but when he got out of sight of anyone who might see him, he turned and headed toward the creek. He took Bert's little dingy and headed east to a place that he had heard his mother speak about. She had talked of a Creole cousin of hers who lived deep in the bayou. He knew that the Creole did not like the clan and that they probably would help him.

He rowed most of the night, making sure that he was out of the area that the people of Swamp Town was familiar with. Hoping that no one would see him, he slept in the boat that night and had planned to search for his Creole family that next day.

It was a dark night. He hid himself in the thickets, tying his boat to a bush to keep it from drifting. He had been used to being alone but not like this night. As the dingy rocked, he sat there, trying to relax but each hoot of the owls startled him. There must have been hundreds of living things around him, each one trying to stay alive. He must have slept for a short time because when he came to his senses, his clothes were damp with the morning dew and the animals were up searching for their breakfast. He quietly raised his head above the side of the boat and peeked out through the tall grass to see what he could see.

It was still so dark that he could hardly see anything. The thick fog rising up from the surface of the water obscured the view beyond the creek's edge. He decided to wait for the sun to come up so that he could see which way to go.

After Sarah left the house, Mrs. Williams and her son sat there in silence for an hour or so. Brenda had gone up to her bedroom and laid down for a nap. Breaking the silence, Mrs. Williams said, "I wonder where Sarah went?"

With those words, Mr. Williams left his house and went straight to a bar.

He just wanted to have a drink and cool off. When he walked into the bar, he heard mumbling at a table where David, Brenda's former boyfriend, was sitting. One of the men saw Mr. Williams and motioned for him to come over.

"Have a seat over here," the man said.

"What's going on?" Mr. Williams asked. His mind was really elsewhere.

"We're talking about going after that Josh," David said. His face was red with anger.

Had they heard about Brenda and Josh's incident? Mr. Williams was thinking how has the news spread this fast? Did Brenda tell someone before she told her mother? What's going on here? He tried to focus on the conversation. "What did you people hear?" he asked.

"We heard that Josh raped Brenda," one of the angry men replied.

Mr. Williams wanted to calm the men. "Well, I'm going to the police and get him to do an investigation. You guys hold tight until I get back with you." He downed his drink and left the bar.

The four men sat at the table. You could still feel the anger in the silence. David finally spoke up. "Why should we wait for the police? John saw them from the bank of the creek." John was the man who was fishing on the opposite side of the creek when the deed was done.

"Yeah, but did he say that he was raping her?" said one of the guys.

David was livid. At that moment, John had entered the bar and was ready to order when he saw David and the others.

"There is John now. Let's ask him if she was being raped," said one of David's friends.

"David downed another bourbon. "John! Come over here," David yelled. "Did you see Josh raping Brenda?"

John was amused. "I saw them making out," John said.

David stood up almost flipping the table. "That's it!" The liquor was fueling the fire. "Let's go get him."

John tried to relax the boys but the drinking had gotten them out of control. "Wait a minute," said John. "I said that they were making out." He could see there was no use. The men left without hearing a word that John had said.

The men got into their cars and headed to Josh's place. They drove up, surrounded the house, calling for Josh to come out. Sarah came to the front porch. Frantically, she cried, "He's not here! I tell you, he is not here!"

They carried their torches, fired their guns scaring Sarah out of her wits. She dropped to her knees praying that the men would go away and leave her son alone. They did not leave until after the house was searched. When they drove away, she heard one of them say, "He's probably over there at that black school in Alabama."

Mr. Williams drove up with the police just as the clan drove away. The police decided to go over to Sarah's house first. The police questioned Sarah about where she thought her son was. She had no intentions of telling him where Josh was, but she knew that the police thought that he was back in school. Mrs. Williams met the police and Mr. Williams on their way back to her house. She invited them in and insisted that Sarah be in on the meeting because she wanted Sarah to hear what Brenda had to tell the police. Brenda's story would improve Josh's chances but first they had to stop the clan.

They needed the truth from Brenda. Marge had returned by that time and saw the police coming toward the home. Mr. Williams was with them and told her that they wanted to interview Brenda.

Still not ready to speak to Mr. Williams, Marge motioned them into the home and called for her daughter from the stairwell. "Come on, Brenda. The police are here to take your statement."

Brenda had no desire to speak to the police. She still had her night clothes on. Coming down the stairs, she was tired and still sobbing. "What kind of statement do you want?" she asked.

The policeman was direct. "I want to ask you if you have been raped."

Brenda was ashamed of being asked that question again. "Why do you want to ask me that, sir?"

He watched her closely. "Some of the people are saying that you were raped by Josh."

Brenda could not keep up with the lies. "If anyone was raped, it was Josh," she said.

"Have you been hurt in any way?" the police asked.

Meekly, she replied, "I have not been raped."

The police turned to her parents and asked, "Are there any other questions?"

"No," said Marge as Mr. and Mrs. Williams silently shook their heads. "Well, that's all I have." The officer had bigger things to be worried about. "Now, I have to get into town and see what those crazy people are doing," the police said.

The next day, Brenda went to Grace's house. Grace walked part of the way down the lane. She knew that Brenda was angry at her for telling David that she was pregnant and that she wanted to say that she was sorry. About half way up the driveway, they met and sat down on a bench under a tree. Her voice was soft and low as she welcomed her friend Brenda.

"I'm so glad that you came by to see me. I wanted to say that I'm sorry that I told David that you were pregnant. He was asking about you and I just let it slip out. Please forgive me."

Brenda was only concerned about Josh. "I'm just so worried about Josh. I wonder where he is."

"David and the men with him thinks that he's gone to that black school," said Grace. "I think that they are going up there after him."

"I hope not," said Brenda. She did not tell Grace that she knew that he was her brother. She got up from the bench and looked back at her friend, no longer angry. She said, "I'm not upset with you, Grace. You are still my best friend."

Grace's smile was a welcome sight for Brenda. This was a good time to have a best friend.

David and his people had gone to the college looking around and asking about a student named Josh. No one would say that they knew him or would admit to knowing him. They came back to Swamp Town, but they did not give up even though the police had told them that there were no charges against him.

They would often meet in the bar and talk about where he might have gone. Periodically, they would watch Sarah and Alice's houses, hoping to catch him going to see them.

Josh had not rested well his first night on the run. He was lost and had no way of telling where he was but now that the sun was up, he knew that he had to go east to find his mother's cousin. His only hope was that if he found them, they would believe him and give him some help. His rowing soon took him to the edge of Lake Pontchartrain. He turned north, staying hidden in the tall grass and keeping an eye out for anything that might give him a clue that would help him to remember something that his mother might have said. It was late in the evening when he realized that he needed to look for a place to tie his boat up. He feared the tall grass would not hold his boat so he looked for trees that would be strong enough to hold the boat and large enough to give him some shade. It was getting late so he rowed his boat into a cove, tied it to a small tree, and then laid down for a little rest.

The place was thick with brush and weeds. The large trees were filled with Spanish moss that hung low over the entrance of the cove. Except for the gators and a few snakes, Josh felt pretty safe. The sound of the water and the wave motion made it easy for him to sleep.

At six o'clock the next morning, Josh was awakened by the sound of movement. He sat up and looked around. He could see more clearly now. The area where he slept showed signs of use by fishermen and there was a path that lead away from the cove.

He decided to go for a walk to see what he could discover. After a quarter of a mile or so, he heard a dog barking and what sounded like the sound of a man working. As Josh walked along, he thought, *Now is no time for fear. I have to find out if these people know anything about my cousin.* He had forgotten that he had his gun on him and did not want to antagonize anyone, but there it was in his belt. It was too late now. From where he stood, he could see that there were two kids on the porch of the house and a man working on a homemade dock close by.

The man called his dogs and spoke to Josh. "How are you doing young man, can I help you?" The man looked at Josh, wondering where he came from and how he got there.

"Yes, sir," Josh said. "I'm a long way from home and I'm lost."

"What's your name?" the man asked.

"I'm Josh."

"Come over and have a seat, I'm Parrot. By the way, did you know that you had a gun?"

"Yes, sir. I'm sorry, sir. Would you like to hold on to it while we talk? I don't want to cause a problem. I didn't want to leave it in the boat and take a chance that some kid might find it."

"It may be a good idea to unload it."

Josh unloaded the gun and sat down as the man had asked. He sat there relaxing by a lean-to shed that was built beside a four-foot-wide dock which extended twenty feet out into the lake. The rear of the lean-to had a one-square-foot opening that was obviously used for hunting ducks.

Mr. Parrot walked over to Josh and asked, "Son, what are you doing lost so far out here in the bayou?"

Josh told Mr. Parrot that he had got into a little trouble and had to get out of town before the clan could get their hands on him, thinking that it would be better to tell the truth than get cough in a lie.

"I see what you mean," Mr. Parrot said. "Those guys don't ask any questions. They just hang you. Why did you come here?"

"My mom said that she had a cousin who lived in this area, so I'm trying to find her to see if I can get some help until I can find out how to get up north."

What is your mother's name?"

Sarah."

"Well, I don't know any Sarah," Mr. Parrot said. "But I'll ask around."

Just then, a young lady came out on the porch with something in her hand. Mr. Parrot, who saw her, called out. "Hey Betty," he said, "I have company. Bring a plate for him." Betty went back into the house and returned with two plates. She gave Josh a plate when she gave her father his plate. Mr. Parrot asked Betty if she knew of a cousin named Sarah.

"No, I don't," she said. "But I think I've heard Mama speak of someone named Sarah a long time ago."

"Ask your mother to come out here when you go back into the house," Parrot told his daughter.

Betty went into the house and told her mother that her father wanted to see her outside. Her mother was just starting to do her house chores.

"What does he want to see me about?" she asked, wanting to begin her work."

"There is a man outside who says that he might be your cousin," Betty said.

Betty's mother, Doris, got up from her chair, took the scarf off her head, and brushed her hair back. "Let me go and see who this is," she said to herself. She walked out onto the porch and peered into the distance, trying to get a good look at this person. All she could see was what looked like a young white man standing there, a little taller than Parrot. She walked closer and closer, moving her head from side to side, trying to see who he was before she got to him. When she got within ten feet of him, she said very slowly, "He does look like someone I used to know."

"He said that his mother's name was Sarah," Parrot said.

"Yes! Yes! He looks like Sarah. He's Sarah's child. My friend Sarah's child. "How is my friend Sarah doing?" She asked Josh.

"She is okay," Josh told her. "She is doing just fine."

Parrot told his wife what Josh had told him about the clan being after him and that he needed a place to hang out while he figure out how to get up north.

"There is no problem. We have to take care of Sarah's child," said Doris.

It had been three days since Josh had seen Alice and his longing for her was growing stronger and stronger. He had to figure out a way to go back and get the one he loved. That afternoon, he went to Mr. Parrot and told him what he planned to do. Mr. Parrot agreed with him saying that he would never leave the one that he loved.

Josh told Mr. Parrot that he was going to get his girl, then he would take his problems and his girl and move on.

Mr. Parrot gave him supplies for his trip which included dried fish, salt pork, and several melons. He also gave him back his gun, fish hooks, and plenty of fishing line. Mr. Parrot said, "After you pick up your girl, go northwest around the lake for about ten miles. When you come to an area at the edge of the lake, where there are some large trees sitting up on a hill, you leave the lake at that point and walk north to a road that goes west to a little town. There is a train that goes north from that little town. If you can catch that train, you will have a good chance of getting up north."

Josh decided to rest one more day before going back to Swamp Town to get his girl, thinking that if he traveled all night and rested the next day, he could get into Swamp Town late the next evening. He wanted to get into town late and meet Alice the next morning when she came out to feed the animals.

Josh rowed into position at about nine thirty, hid the boat a hundred feet from where it was normally kept, and swam to the shore. He laid there for an hour or so, making sure that no one was around. Later he went to the barn, climbed up to the loft, and went to sleep in the hay.

Josh slept until about four the next morning. He was wide awake at that time and waiting for Alice to come out to the barn. It was a foggy morning as usual in that area so close to the creek. The sun was not yet up when Josh heard metal bumping against something and the squeaking of a bucket as it does when it is being carried by a person who is walking. He stood there, being very quiet, trying to see who was coming toward him. At first he saw an outline of a person, then someone wearing a skirt. At last, he could tell that it was Alice. Still he kept quiet, making sure that no one was following her.

Alice came in as she usually did, putting the bridle on the cow and leading her to the milking station, then she sat down to milk the cow.

Josh called her name very quietly. "Alice," he said. She did not hear him at first then he called again; this time, a little louder. She heard him but could not tell where the voice was coming from. She looked around, trying to see where he was. She walked a few steps from the cow, moving toward the sound.

He called again. "Alice, I'm up here." Josh stopped for a minute. "Keep milking, I think I heard someone coming," he said.

"It's my father," Alice whispered. "He's coming to feed the animals."

Josh relaxed a bit. "Okay," Josh said. "I'll just lay here until he leaves."

Alice continued milking the cow.

Her father called to her. "Go up to the loft and throw some hay down into the mule stalls."

"Okay," I'll be right there." Alice tried to remain calm. She climbed up to the loft to throw the hay down. Whispering to Josh, she said, "He is not coming up here now. When I'm finish, I'll come back and talk with you."

After finishing her chores, Alice went back to the house. Her father was already in the house getting ready for breakfast. Alice sat down at the table.

Mavis, her mother, noticed her daughter's quietness.

"What's on your mind?" Mavis asked as she began setting the breakfast table.

"Why do you ask?" Alice replied.

"Because you look like the cat that ate the canary, I can see a smile all over your face." What's going on?" her mother said.

"Not much," Alice said. "I'll tell you this afternoon."

"I'll be working in the east end cotton field today," her father said. He asked Alice to give him his dinner box. Alice got the dinner box off the table behind her and took it to her father at the door. He went back to the barn, hooked the mule up to the cart, and headed to the east end cotton field.

Alice helped her mother with the dishes and making the beds. When she was done, she went back to the barn to see what was on Josh's mind. Josh remained in the loft, waiting for her to come to where he was. She climbed up the ladder and sat down on a bale of hay. Hugging him tightly, she squeezed and kissed him. "Now," she said. "Tell me what's going on."

"I had to get away before the clan came," Josh said.

"Why did you come back here?"

"I have decided to go up north and I want you to come with me."

Alice was taken by surprise. "I don't know, Josh. I don't even know where that is."

Josh was adamant. "I can't live here and I don't know what I would do without you. I'm so scared. I don't know what to do." He couldn't stand it any longer. "I have to go, honey! I don't want to but I have to."

"I have to talk with my mother," Alice told him. "If I'm not back by nine, I won't have the nerve to go. So please wait till then." She held his hands and kissed him, then went back to the house.

Mavis knew her daughter was keeping secrets. "Where have you been?" her mother asked when Alice returned.

"I was out at the barn," Alice said nervously.

"I thought that you had finished your work out there? I want you to start the wash, you know today is Friday," her mother said.

Alice was still standing by her mother's side, but she did not know how to tell her mother what she had to tell her. Mavis wanted to make it easier for her.

"What is it," Her mother asked. "What do you have to tell me?"

Alice spoke, hanging onto to every word, "Josh...Josh is in the barn."

Mavis eyes grew wide. "Do you mean Sarah's son? Does she know that he's here? What does he want?"

Alice was waiting for that question, and with an outburst of emotion, she shouted, "He wants me to go with him."

Mavis would have none of this. "No no no," her mother cried. "I don't want you to get mixed up in this mess."

Alice sat down in a chair by the kitchen door. She looked up at her mother with tears flowing down from her eyes. "I've got to go with him," she said softly. I just got to go. I'm so sorry, Mama. I just got to go." Her decision was made.

Mavis knew she had to accept it. "Wait a moment, baby," her mother said. "I think that his mother should know that he is here. I'll go over and tell her."

It was now eight thirty in the morning and Sarah was just finishing the breakfast dishes. Mavis was walking swiftly toward the Williams's kitchen, but she had not made up her mind how to tell Sarah without letting the Williamses know what was going on. She rushed into the kitchen where Sarah was and motioned her out to the porch.

Sarah rushed to her side, wondering what in the world was wrong. "What is it?" Sarah asked.

"Sarah, your boy's chickens are all over my garden. Come over and help me get them out of my place." She was waving both of her hands trying to get her attention.

Mrs. Williams was sitting in the living room and heard the commotion. She came to the door, saw Mavis and gave a little smile.

"You had better hurry up, Sarah, before they eat up all of her vegetables."

Sarah rushed out of the kitchen, then the two of them, headed for Mavis's garden. Once out of Mrs. Williams's sight, Mavis slowed her pace. "Wait a minute," Mavis said, slowing to a walking pace. "Let me get my breath! There is no problem with the chickens. I've got something to tell you." The two of them were walking more slowly now. Mavis with her hands on her hips was breathing a little better now.

Sarah was confused. "What is it then?"

Mavis leaned a little closer to Sarah's ear and said, "Josh is in the barn."

"Oh! Lord!" Sarah screamed. "Josh! Josh!" Sarah could not control her excitement. "Where is my boy?" Sarah ran to the barn with her arms in the air streaming. "Where are you? Josh! Where is my boy?"

Josh heard her screams and came to the door. He could not keep the tears from falling when he saw his mother. "Mom, Mom, is that you?" He said. "I'm up here! Mom, I'm in the barn."

She reached out to him. "It's me, baby. Are you all right?" She cried.

I'm okay. But not so loud, someone may be listening."

Sarah tried to lower her voice. She was overcome with excitement. "I'm so glad that you came to see me. What are you planning to do?" Sarah was concerned and afraid for her boy.

"I'm going up north," he said. "But first, I've got to get away from here."

Mavis was on their front porch, watching to see if anyone was around while Alice was in the house gathering things that she thought she might need.

"I found your cousin in the bayou," Josh told his mother. "They helped me out. They gave me a place to rest, food, and some advice on how to get to a place to catch a train going north."

"How are you going to get to the train?" his mother asked.

"They say that on the far side of the lake, there is a road that goes to a place where the train stops. If I can get there and if I can get on the train, I'm on my way up north, but first I've got to get out of here."

Sarah squeezed his fingers. It was hard to let go. "Let me know where you are. Send me a letter but don't send it to me, send it to Jesse Mae. She will get it to me."

Josh hesitated for a moment, then he said, "Mom, go and see if Alice is going with me."

His mother couldn't help but smile. "She is going, Josh. I know she's going."

Josh was relieved. "Tell her I have to leave at nine."

Sarah left Josh with tears in her eyes and hope in her heart. When she got to Mavis's house, she could see that Alice was ready to leave, so she wished them well.

Sarah went back to work. She knew that Mrs. Williams wanted and needed to know that Josh was all right. After all, he was her grandson, but she would have to wait until he was well on his way out of town.

When Sarah walked into the kitchen, Mrs. Williams asked, "Did you get all of the chickens locked up?"

"Yes," Sarah said. "We took care of everything." She went back to work.

CHAPTER 10

As soon as she could, Alice got all of their traveling gear together and put it in a pile near the boat. She had made up her mind not to tell her father. She would leave that for her mother to do. At eight forty–five, she walked out of her house for the last time. Alice headed for the barn where Josh was waiting. It was nine o'clock. She called up to the loft and watched as Josh carefully climbed down. Once down, he saw Bert's fishing gear which had been there since he had died. He saw a knife that had been used for cleaning fish, hanging on a nail, and took it from its resting place, tucked it in his belt, and rushed out of the barn to catch up with Alice.

Alice was wearing a blue jean coat, blue jean pants, a Panama-style straw hat, and high top sneakers. She carried a foot tub filled with sweet potatoes, hard tacks, canned beans, and two quarts of water.

When Josh got to the boat, they loaded their gear, untied the boat, and headed back up the creek to Lake Pontchartrain. They rowed quietly up the creek through the water lilies and wire grass and on past the knoll where young lovers were known to hang out. That night, the knoll was occupied by David and his new girlfriend, Grace.

Grace and David were enjoying each other when Grace suddenly stopped. "I thought I heard something," Grace said.

David sat up and turned his ear toward the creek. "Yeah," he said quietly. "I think someone is out there and it must be that Josh. Let's go," he said. Grabbing Grace by the arm, David jumped up, ran to his car, and they sped away.

Josh had heard the car and a slight fear came over him, but he had to keep to his plan, knowing that David would have to take some time to get his clan together. By then, maybe, just maybe he would have time to get away.

David was heading toward the town bar where he planned to get a couple of other guys to join him in his hunt for Josh.

Grace was nervous. "What are you going to do, David?" Grace asked.

He looked at her in disbelief. "I'm going to get him. I'm going to get that nigger." She could see the dark hatred in his eyes.

"You are mad," Grace said. "He has not even been charged with anything."

"I don't care," David replied. "I want to get him for what he did." Not wanting to be a part of it, Grace told David to drop her off at her house.

David took her home and dropped her off without saying a word. After he dropped her off, David returned to the bar. He rushed in and saw Brock and Al sitting at a table, having a drink of rum.

Al could see that he was all keyed up. "What's up?" Al asked.

David was livid. "I saw him," he said, while he paced with anger. "I saw that boy Josh. He was out there in the creek. He had been to see that black girl and was sneaking back to where he was staying. Come on you guys, let's go out there and see if we can get him."

Al sipped his drink. He saw his friend's anger, but he said, "I'm not going out there hunting for a man that has not been charged of any crime."

David's anger never wavered. "Damn, Al," He said. "You some kind of a coward?"

Al was not convinced. "I'm just not going out there in that damn creek, looking for a man that has not been charged of anything," Al said.

David looked at Al with disgust and turned to the other drinker. "Come on, man." He said to Brock. Reluctantly, Brock followed the angry man.

The two men got in David's car. They stopped at David's house and got his boat. "We'll put the boat in the creek on the west side of Jesse's place, then we'll row all the way to the knoll and see if we can find him."

"Okay," said Brock. They hooked the boat to his car and headed up the path that paralleled the creek's edge in an effort to cut off Josh before he got too far. When they got to the creek, David said, "This is where the deed was done. We'll put the boat in the water here and row toward the knoll and see if we can find him."

Josh had gotten to the spot where he had stopped for rest on his way to the bayou. At this point, the water was over two feet deep. He and Alice took turns rowing, keeping as close to the tall grass as possible. The two of them pulled their boat into the tallest and thickest grass they could find and stopped to take a break. They listened quietly for any sound that might be in the area. Satisfied, they settled down for a little rest.

At about 2:45 a.m., Josh thought that he heard something and sat up to see if he could detect any movement.

Alice slowly sat up and said, "I think I hear something, too."
Josh told her to be quiet. "I hear it, too. Just keep quiet and
stay low in the boat," he whispered.

There was a large cypress stump located about twenty feet away
with several cypress tree knees sticking up just above the water
level. Josh slid like a giant snake into the water and emerged on
the grassy side of the tree stump. He took some Spanish moss
that hung from a nearby tree and wrapped it around his shoulders
and head, then climbed up on the grassy side of the stump and sat
there waiting to see what was making the noise.

About fifteen minutes later, he saw what he thought was a
boat with two men in it. "They must be after me," he said to himself. There is no other reason for anyone to be out here this time
of the night. The men crept closer and closer. Josh noticed the
men were keeping an eye on the bank of the creek. He heard one
of them say, "They may be over there taking a nap.

They are looking for me on the bank, Josh thought. They rowed
within three feet of the cypress stump that Josh had climbed
onto. Josh could see that the men had a shotgun and a Colt .45.
The man at the front of the boat was David, but he did not know
who the other man was. He heard David say, "I'm going to get
that black bastard if it's the last thing I do." Josh could wait no
longer. He jumped. All of his weight came down on the port side
and aft end of the boat. The bow came up, throwing David out of
the boat. When he came down, his head hit the top of one of the
cypress knees. Josh saw David sank to the bottom.

Josh remembering that he had his gun in his belt, so before
he came up out of the water, he reached for it. When he came up
out of the water, he had the gun in his hand, but the second man
was scrambling, trying to get to safety at the creek's bank. Their
boat was overturned. Josh dived back to the bottom, searching
for the shotgun but no luck. Josh swam back over to his boat and
climbed back in without saying a word.

Alice took the oars and started rowing. She rowed completely
out of the creek. They turned northwest and kept as close to the

edge of the lake's coast as possible. They rowed for a mile or so before the sun came up, then they found a place with high grass, cattails, and a few small trees. Figuring this was a safe place, they tied up their boat and tried to get some sleep.

The two of them had been very quiet and had rested for most of the day, saying nothing since the incident in the creek. The sun was now going down and the two of them had decided to row in the late evening and the early morning. Before they started rowing, Alice looked into Josh's eyes and asked, "What in the world happened in the creek."

Josh couldn't look at her. "It was that boy David and some other man. They were talking about killing me. They had a shotgun, and when the man in the rear of the boat looked around, he reached for the gun. So I jumped into the boat. I don't know what happened after that."

After rowing for about an hour, they came to a place where the border of the lake was void of bush and grass. The property belonged to a farmer who had built a dock. A few hundred feet away was the farmer's house, and they could hear the barking of a dog. Before they realized it, they were out in the open. Alice lay down on the floor of the boat, but Josh sat up straight as if he was just out for a little exercise and no one seemed to notice. They continued on for two days and nights. Fishing a little to keep themselves busy.

Early that next morning, Alice saw an area just beyond the edge of the water that looked like a small island. They rowed over as close to it as they could.

"That's solid dry land," Josh said. "Let's go over and see if we can set up camp for the night."

"That sound like a good idea," Alice told him. "I want to see if I can still walk."

They rowed over as close as possible, got out of the boat, pulled it on to dry land, and tied it to a fallen tree limb. The elevated area was about two feet above the lake surface and covered about five hundred square yards. Alice was so happy to be on solid ground that she ran around the area, trying to loosen up her stiff joints. Josh joined her.

Their food was getting low, but they still had some of the sweet potatoes that Alice had brought along. Josh built a fire out of some dead branches that were lying around, then he placed two large green branches over the fire and placed the potatoes on them to cook before the green branches burned to the point that they wouldn't support anything. He got his fishing gear and found some grubs under the dead tree limbs and went fishing. Catching sunfish, catfish, and some crabs.

Alice explored the island finding grapes, maypops, and huckleberries. They had the fish and berries for that afternoon and saved the crabs for the next day. The weather was dry and warm, and they had plenty to eat so they spent two days and three nights at this place, resting, washing their clothes, and relaxing in the warm sun by the lake.

That third night, Josh said to Alice, "We must leave this place soon." He kept looking for those trees on that hill.

"I know," she said. "But I was beginning to like it here."

Josh could see her contentment. "I know," he said reluctantly. "But we have to go before someone finds us here." The next morning, before the sun came up, they left their cozy little island.

As they rowed northwest around the lake, it wasn't long before Josh saw in the distant a clump of trees that look like they were above the lake level as Parrot had told him they would be. He pointed toward the trees and said to Alice, "That's where we are going. I hope that that's near to where the road that leads to the train station so that we won't have to be far to walk."

Alice sat in the bow of the boat, looking at the spot that Josh had pointed out to her. She had no way of telling how far they had to go, but she was relaxed now and was ready for the task. They were following the edge of the lake as they had planned but now they had come to a point where the lake jutted out into the land mass further than the eye could see. To follow the edge in this situation may take more than two or three days. The only other thing that they could do was to go straight across that part of the lake. So they headed out into deep water.

It was early in the morning and they both had eaten a good meal. Josh would row first. They headed straight for the clump of trees. The sun was hot and the waves in the deeper waters tossed them around like a leaf in a pond.

Alice grew restless, shifting her body around, letting her feet hang over the side of the boat, cooling them off in the waves off the lake. The cool water on her feet felt so good so she splashed water on her body and later, she started splashing the cool water on Josh's body, cooling him off as well.

Josh could see the clump of trees as if they were planted there to act as a lighthouse just for him, calling him to come and be rescued. With that vision in his mind, he rowed and rowed on and on into the night until his exhaustion overcame him. The night folded around him and gave him comfort, and he drifted away into a sound sleep.

Alice also slept and dreamed of flowers and beautiful things. They were left all alone in this big lake with only the angels to look after them. They slumbered and knew not where they were or how long they slept. When they awakened, their first thought was that they were in the middle of the lake. They were heartbroken, thinking that they had drifted to the center of Lake Pontchartrain. The fog was thick and laying low on the lake. Visibility was close to nothing. They sat there hungry, wet, and lost, wondering how much work they would have to do to get back to civilization.

They were sitting there, facing the starboard side of the boat when the orange rays of the sun lit up the sky. The sun popped up over the horizon bringing in a new day. Josh said slowly to himself, "The sun rises in the east…" They were facing the east.

"Then we were heading northwest."

Then the both of them turned around and there, standing before them, was the clump of trees a few hundred feet away, just like what Mr. Parrot had said it would be. The bank of the coast was about ten feet high and very steep so after they reached the edge of the lake, they rowed about a hundred feet along the coastline and found an area that they could use to easily climb out of the lake. The splashing of the waves had exposed the tree roots so that they could grab hold of them and pull themselves up from the lake.

Alice climbed out first. When she got to level ground, she flopped to the ground on her butt, drew her legs up to her chest, and folded her arms over her knees. She placed her head on her arms and tried to get some rest. She was hungry, tired, and her body ached from sitting on a small bench rowing a boat for days and days. Her body was spent and void of any energy. To add to her problems on the ground twenty feet away, a copperhead came slithering in her direction.

Alice made a decisive decision and said to herself, "If you don't bother me, I won't bother you." Sitting there, not moving but watching to see if the snake would make the wrong move. The snake came within a foot of her, flicking its tongue and deciding that she was not his type.

Josh took time to pick out the things from the boat that he thought he might need. Then he tied the boat to the root of a tree and climbed onto the bank. By this time, the snake was gone. Josh looked around the area. There was a path that followed the edge of the lake and one that ran between two cornfields leading away from the lake.

Josh walked over to the cornfield and got two ears of corn, hoping that the corn would not be too hard to eat. The corn was hard but not too hard for a hungry man to eat. The more they chewed the raw corn, the easier it was to consume. With their stomach full, they lay there with their heads on their belongings and went to sleep.

They must have been there for two hours when Josh opened his eyes. The sun was well above the horizon. They could see clearly now that they were on a farm because there were many signs of mules and carts throughout the area. Alice opened her eyes, stretched and got up. "I think I heard someone," she said. Josh stood to his feet and looked around. There in the distant was a man walking their way. It was a black man who seemed to be just going for a walk. He walked right up to Josh who had the gun in his belt.

"How are you young people doing?" he asked.

"I'm fine," Josh said warily. "This is my friend Alice."

Alice softly said, "Hello."

"I'm Frank Baker," the man said. "Are you people lost?"

"Yes," Josh said. "Sir, we are very lost."

"I believe you," the man said, looking at Josh. "I see that you have a gun."

"Yes, sir," Josh agreed. "But we have no intention of harming anyone. And to show you that I mean what I'm saying. I'd like for you to take the gun so you want have to worry about it."

Frank took the gun and then said, "Come with me to the house where we can sit and talk."

CHAPTER 11

THEY WALKED OVER to the path that led away from the lake. Alice's legs were still shaken from being away from solid ground so long. She lagged behind the two men who said very little on the way to the house.

The house was a beautiful bungalow with a large front porch and beautiful flowers all around it. On the left side of the path was a large two-story pack house with a lean-to shed on one end and a barn on the other end. Under the lean-to was a wagon, cart, and plows. On the west side of the pack house was a fenced-in area with five goats, three mules, and a cow. At the rear of the backyard was a large chicken coup with chicken and ducks inside the fenced-in area.

The three of them walked around to the front porch. Mr. Baker sat on the swing and placed the gun on the swing beside him. Josh and Alice sat on chairs next to the swing. Mr. Baker looked at the two young people and asked, "Where are you two young people going?"

Josh felt that he could open up and talk to this man. "We are trying to get up north." Josh said.

"Have you ever been up north?" Mr. Baker asked.

"No," said Josh.

"Well, it's a long way off and it gets pretty cold up there." Mr. Baker said. Looking at them, he added, "Have you people ever worked on a farm?"

"Yes," they both said in unison.

"I have been thinking that if the two of you could stay around a while, let's say until spring. You could earn a few dollars and leave for up north after the cold weather is over."

"That sound like a good idea!" Josh replied. He turned to Alice and asked, "What do you think, Alice?"

"I think that's a great idea but where will we sleep?" she asked.

Frank got up from his seat and went to the door of the house. "Martha," he called.

A voice came from one of the inner rooms. "What is it, Frankie?"

"Come out on the porch. We have company."

A few minutes later, a handsome brown-skinned woman, about five feet eight inches with a beautiful head full of hair pulled back into a ponytail, walked briskly out on to the porch. She went directly to Alice, giving her a hug all the time welcoming her and then she went toward the swing to sit down; she saw the gun. "What's that thing doing there?" she asked her husband.

"Oh, that belonged to them. They gave it to me to show their trust."

Martha looked at it with disgust. "Well, put it away. We don't need it laying around out here."

Frank took the gun. "I'm going to put it in the closet until you are ready for it," he said to Josh, who introduced himself and Alice.

"Glad to meet you," Mrs. Baker said pleasantly. "How did you meet my Frankie?"

"We were down by the lake and Mr. Baker just walked up and said hello. We told him that we were lost and could use a little help." Alice had told her a lot of the truth but not enough to disturb them.

Mr. Baker came back out on the porch and sat down on the swing beside his wife.

"Martha," he said. "I was talking to Josh and Alice about helping us with the harvest this year. They think it's a good idea, but they will need some place to stay."

"The place would not have to be much," Josh added. "Just some where a person could get some sleep."

Martha glanced at the couple. "I have to ask a question," she said. "Are you two people married?"

"No," Alice answered. "And we don't mind you asking the question."

"In that case," Mrs. Baker said. "I have a solution. Alice can stay in the house with me and you can fix up the room attached to the pack house for Josh." She looked at Frankie for approval. "What do you think?"

Frank asked the couple what they thought.

"I think it will be just fine." Josh smiled. "What about you?" he asked Alice, and she agreed.

"One other thing," Frank said. "I don't have a lot of cash on hand, so you can eat with us and I can pay you at the end of harvest time. If you agree to this, we can go to work on that room."

Josh was amazed at their good fortune. "That is the best offer that I have had in a long time," Josh replied.

"Come with me," Martha said to Alice.

When they got to the kitchen, Martha showed Alice two baskets of apples, a basket of peaches and one of grapes. She looked at Alice and said, "We are going to can all of this food for the winter. If you don't mind learning something, I'll teach you how to do it all."

Alice looked at Mrs. Baker and a smile covered her entire face. She was beginning to like this lady and was very happy that she was offering to teach her how to do these things.

Mr. Baker took Josh out to the room at the end of the pack house. It was a twelve-by-ten-foot room that was being used for storage. Mr. Baker told Josh that everything in that room could be stored up stairs while he was there. The frame of a bunk bed was in place and Josh was given some slats for his bunk, a chair, and a table.

By the time, Josh got the stored items relocated and the slats installed in his bed, Mrs. Baker and Alice were standing there with his mattress and bedding.

The ladies put the bedding on the floor and said, "We'll see you later, Josh. Mrs. Baker and I have some canning to do." Alice was getting along wonderfully with Mrs. Baker, so much so, it made her feel good. Josh didn't feel so bad himself, fixing up his room and feeding the animals.

It had been a week and a half since anyone had seen or heard from David and the man who had left the bar with him. When Grace heard people talking of this, she started asking around. She had hesitated to ask Brenda since he had been her boyfriend. But later, Grace asked Brenda if she had seen David lately.

"No," Brenda said. "I thought you were seeing David."

Grace did not know that Brenda was aware of her seeing her former boyfriend.

"Grace," Brenda said. "Do you think that I'm upset that you are seeing David?"

"I didn't know," Grace said. "I thought that you were through with him."

Brenda was not angry. "I am through with him and I'm still friends with you."

Grace was relieved. "Thank you. I'm so happy that we are still good friends. Let's go to the bar and have a cold one."

The two girls were sitting in the bar, reminiscing about the fun that they used to have in the pool. One of the guys who used to hang around with David saw them and came over to their table. He sat down beside Grace.

"Have you girls seen David around lately?" he asked.

"That's odd. We were just about to ask you about him," Brenda said.

That question got around and soon the police was interested in where the two men were. After questioning the people in the town, the police decided to search the area. But first, the police had to ask Grace a few questions because the news of her being at the knoll with David had gotten around town as well.

The police showed up at Grace's house that next afternoon. Her father who had heard of the concern for the missing men was very upset that the police had the nerve to come to his house.

He met the police at their car in the yard before they came to the door. "Why are you coming in my yard?" Grace's father asked in a hushed voice.

"No problem," the police calmed Grace's father down. "We just want to ask her a few questions. She is not in any trouble."

Grace's father was not convinced. "I'll go get her," he said. He went into his house and in a few minutes, Grace appeared and walked over to the police car.

She did not appear nervous. "What can I do for you?" she asked.

The police were direct. "When was the last time you saw David?"

"It was a week and a half ago."

"And where were you at that time?"

"We were at the knoll in Swamp Town."

"Did anything unusual happen?"

"He said that he thought he heard something in the creek."

"Did he say what it was?"

Grace remained calm. "No."

"What did he do then?"

"He said that he thought the noise was Josh." Grace felt a lump in her throat, thinking that it might have been Josh.

"And what happened next?"

"He dropped me off at my house and said that he was going to the bar and get someone to go with him to get that Josh."

The officers left and Grace finally relaxed. The next stop for the police was at Brenda's house. They asked Brenda all the usual questions but got no information because she had not seen David for weeks. She did however mention that she and David had also been at the knoll a couple of months earlier. The police decided to search the knoll and a section of the creek.

The search started at the end of the creek where Josh did a lot of fishing. The two policemen rowed the boat up the creek, looking for anything that might look suspicious. Thirty minutes had passed before they reached the large cypress stumps. They searched around the stumps, through the tall grass then moved over to the other side of the creek.

"Hold up," said one of the searchers. "I think I see something. Look over there, under that bush." He said "There is something red under there."

"I see it," the other man said. They rowed the boat closer and closer. No one uttered a word. They both feared what they might find. When the police chief pulled away the branch that blocked his view, they found a body wedged under it. Ted, the youngest one of the searchers said. That's him. That's the man David was with.

They pulled Brock out of the creek and later found David wedged under the root of a cypress tree. Their boat was found overturned a few yards from the site but no signs of any other boat. The case was left open, pending any evidence that might be found at a later date.

Josh and Alice had been at the Baker's home for three weeks and Josh had helped Mr. Baker with the livestock while Alice had been very helpful in the kitchen with Mrs. Baker. The next week was the beginning of harvest time for cotton and corn. At this part of the harvest time, four groups of farmers worked together. When they worked on the Baker's farm, the lady of the house prepared food for breakfast, lunch, and dinner for all of the people involved.

Alice had gotten used to working with Mrs. Baker so when she was asked to stay in the kitchen to help her, she jumped at the chance.

Josh joined the men who went to the field to gather corn. It took him a while to get used to the job, but he caught on quickly. The work was hard and the hours were long but the men were friendly and no one asked him where he came from or where he was going. In the afternoon, when the work was done, some of the men gathered at the house next door and played checkers. Josh, who had played a little bit of checkers with his friend Jack and the Jones brothers, was asked to come over and play with them. He went over and joined the group and though his game was not that good, he was accepted in the group as one of them.

Alice spent a lot of time in the kitchen with Mrs. Baker but when cotton picking time came, she went to the cotton fields. It was hard for her to catch on, but in a group of the younger people, she kept up pretty good. Everyone was working at their own pace and the people were good to her, but after a few days, she was longing to be working with Mrs. Baker.

It was getting close to Thanksgiving time and Mrs. Baker was preparing food for the church dinner, so she called on her favorite helper and Alice was glad to get back in the kitchen. Josh and Mr. Baker was busy pulling fodder for the animals to eat and preparing the ground for the new crops.

Christmas would be coming soon and after that they would be planting corn, wheat, and soy beans, and it would be time for the young couple to head up north.

Mr. Baker was really proud of having this young couple around, but he would soon have to let them go. The last two weeks passed by in a hurry with Josh shelling corn with the mechanical corn shelling machine and Alice was spending a lot more time with Josh, helping him bag the corn to be sold at the miller's shop.

The next week was the time for the young couple to go up north so Josh and Alice told the Bakers when they were planning to leave.

Mr. Baker didn't really want to see them go, but a promise is a promise so he said to them, "I'll go to the bank and get your money."

"Thank you," Josh said. "Will you stop by the train station and get our tickets?" Josh was still being careful and not wanting to be seen.

"Of course, I will," the older man replied.

Mr. Baker knew that the other men and Josh had become good friends, so he asked them if they would give Josh a going away night out, down at the bar near the farm.

They all agreed, so the guys picked Josh up that evening and took him to the bar for a couple of beers. The place was similar to the place that Jesse Mae owned so Josh felt relaxed. That night, a guitar player was on the stage playing the blues. All of the girls in the place were known by the fellows who were with Josh, and they tried to give Josh a good time by dancing with him. The outing was uneventful except the guitar player thought that he recognized Josh but said nothing about it.

That next morning, Mrs. Baker and Alice were sitting in the swing on the porch. Josh walked up and sat in the chair facing them. He offered his good mornings.

"Did you get a good night's rest? Mrs. Baker asked.

"Yes, ma'am, I did," Josh answered.

Mr. Baker came out onto the porch. "Good morning to all," he said and sat down beside Josh. He had a piece of paper in his hand that he gave to Josh. "See if these figures are right," Mr. Baker said. "Then give it to Alice."

Josh checked the figures. "Yep, they are okay by me," he said then he gave the paper to Alice.

Alice checked the paper, agreed and gave the paper back to Mr. Baker.

Mr. Baker then paid Josh and Alice according to their agreement and gave Josh his gun as he said he would do. Josh thanked them both and told them how thankful he was for their help. Alice did the same. Martha felt a tear form in her eye, so she turned and walked into the kitchen. Alice followed her. Mrs. Baker continued walking until she was out by the chicken yard. When they finally came together, there were tears in both of their eyes. They hugged and kissed each other then silently Alice turned and walked away. When Alice turned for that last wave, she saw Mrs. Baker walking down the path that brought them to this little patch of heaven.

Some of the friends that they had met came to see them off. They said their last good-byes at the Baker's home. Mr. Baker took them to the train station and as he dropped them off and after he got back into the car, he said without turning to face them. "If you ever come back this way, you've got a job here." With that, he drove away.

Josh and Alice boarded the train and were on their way up to the north. They had always thought of going up north but on their tickets, the destination was Chicago. Mr. Baker, who knew that all the new people who had gone up north had bought a ticket to Chicago, so that's what he bought for them.

CHAPTER 12

IT HAD BEEN a few weeks since Jesse Mae had had a guitar player in her place. This guitar player was playing the same blues that he had played that night that Josh was celebrating with his friends. The guitar player and Josh were in the same place at the same time. And it would not have meant a thing if those girls had not kept calling out his name. "Josh...Josh," they would call out. "Come and dance with me." There were lots of dancing and joking, and with all of it, with and about the man called Josh. This musician was playing some real down home blues, the girls were doing the slow drag, with their heads pressed against their partner's shoulder, and Josh being six feet tall had stood out among the rest of the crowd.

This night, the same guitar player was at Jesse Mae's place. He was playing the same kind of music and Josh's old friends were dancing with the girls the same way that Josh had danced with the girl in Springfield. When someone mentioned Josh's name, someone else uttered the statement, "I wonder what my man Josh is doing now." It was then that someone heard the guitar player say, "He's probably in Springfield dancing his butt off." The crowd had a good laugh and it seemed as if it would have ended there but within two days, the news was at the police station." Someone had said they heard someone say," Josh was in Springfield. The guitar player did not intend for the word to get out, but when he spoke the words, it spread like wildfire.

Now that Josh was seen in Springfield, the sheriff would have to look for him and to question him about the incident at the creek. But first he wanted to talk to Brenda and her father. He called the Williams's house and asked Mrs. Williams to have her son, Robert, to give the sheriff a call.

About nine o'clock that next evening, the phone in the sheriff's office rang, the sheriff picked up the phone.

"This is Robert Williams," the caller said.

"Hello, Mr. Williams. This is the sheriff. How are you doing today?"

"I'm fine. What can I help you with today?

"Well, Mr. Williams," I got word today that that boy Josh was seen in Springfield a few days ago. Do you think that we should go over there and pick him up and question him?"

Mr. Williams had figured that the incident was over, that the men had drowned by accident. And why was he being asked to go with the sheriff to Springfield. "Why should we talk to Josh, Sheriff? Brenda has already said that he did not rape her."

"Well, sir," said the sheriff, "we don't really have to talk to Brenda. I just thought that I might find out something about those two boys who got drowned in the creek."

"What do you want me to do, Sheriff?" asked Mr. Williams.

"How about riding over to Springfield with me tomorrow. I'm going over there to ask a few people a few questions?"

"Okay," said Mr. Williams. "I'll be ready when you get here."

When Mr. Williams put the phone down, his mother asked, "What did the sheriff want?"

"He heard that Josh was seen in Springfield and he wants me to go over there with him, while he asked a few questions," said Robert.

"Why can't they just leave that boy alone?" Mrs. Williams said. "We have had enough trouble."

"I'll go with him," Robert said. "But I don't know what help I can give him."

The sheriff showed up at the Williams's house at about nine o'clock. Springfield was not much more than a crossroad. The railroad people had expected that it would grow into a large city, but nothing ever happened, all of the commerce went over to Baton Rouge, leaving Springfield with a train station and a few small stores.

"How are you doing this morning?" the Sheriff asked Mr. Williams.

"I'm fine," Robert Williams said. "How long do you think it will be before we get back?"

"Oh, it want be long. I'm just going to the place where he was last seen and ask around a bit. If you have any questions, feel free to ask them."

"Okay, but I have not thought of any so far," said Mr. Williams. They went around the west side of the lake, using a road that had not seen very much traffic and had not ever been paved.

"How far is Springfield?" Mr. Williams asked after they had been on the road for twenty minutes or so.

"It's about fifteen or twenty miles," the Sheriff said. "I hope you don't mind me asking, but how is your wife taking this thing about her daughter and that Josh, suppose they have a baby?"

Mr. Williams wanted to scream. He wanted to yell to the top of his voice, to cry out, to tell the world his entire story, but he held it in. This story could never get out. It would destroy his whole world. His frontal lobe overcame the dark secrets hiding in the interior of his brain and brought him back to reality. "Oh," he said. "Marge is all right but she's been very quiet lately."

They passed a five-mile sign and the sheriff looked at Williams and said. "We have just five more miles to go. We should be there in about fifteen or twenty minutes." When they got about two miles from the place, Mr. Williams said. "Do you think these people will give you any information that you can use?"

"I hope so, but you can't tell. You know most of the people in that town are colored," said the sheriff, considering the way that we have been treating them, you can never tell."

"What do you mean, sir?" Mr. Williams asked the Sheriff. "You have got to know that they know that it was the clan that was after Josh."

"I know, "said the sheriff. "But I'm not the clan."

"Don't fool yourself," Sheriff. "They think that we are all the clan."

"Well," said the sheriff. "We have to try." The two men walked into the only black-owned bar in the small town of Springfield. It was about three o'clock in the afternoon and the place was nearly empty. Three customers in the place were obviously nervous and left the place right away. The bartender and owner held there place behind the bar.

The sheriff said," Good evening, gentlemen, I'm the sheriff of Swamp Town and I would like to ask you a few questions?

The two men stood there quietly, waiting for the question.

"Do you know of a young man named Josh?"

"No," said the first man.

The second man put his hand to his head as if he was trying to think, "No," he said. "I don't know anyone named Josh."

The answer from the only two men seen on the street was the same and they all may have been telling the truth. One man said that he had heard of a stranger who had been working in the cotton field on the Baker's farm.

"Where is the Baker's farm? asked the sheriff.

"I'm not sure," said the man. "You might want to ask the clerk in the train station."

The sheriff decided to take a run over to the Baker's farm, so they asked the clerk at the train station for the location of the Baker's farm. The clerk was very helpful and knew the Bakers very well. The clerk came out of the train station with the offers and pointed to the road that went east and told them, "Go three miles down this road and his house will be a white house with black shutters on the right side of the road."

The ride to the Baker's farm was very short. When they arrived at the Baker's house, Mr. and Mrs. Baker were on the porch sitting in the swing when the police car pulled up. The Bakers continued their restful swinging.

Mr. Baker said, "Y'all, get out of the car and have a seat up here on the porch."

The two of them got out of the car and walked up on the porch and sat down without saying a word.

"How are you doing?" Mr. Baker said.

"We are doing okay," the sheriff said.

"This is a well-kept farm."

"What can I do for you?"

"We are just going around asking if anyone has seen or heard of any one named Josh."

"What did he look like?"

"He was about six feet tall and had very light skin."

"There were a few people who came by here to pick cotton, but my wife and I don't pay that much attention to who's out there working in the fields anymore."

"I can understand that," said Mr. Williams. It's easy to miss someone when you are not looking for them.

"Yeah," said the sheriff.

"Is this your place?" asked Mr. Williams.

"Yes." answered Mr. Baker.

"Do you mind if I take a look around?"

"Not at all," said Mr. Baker.

"I'm just going to set here and have a nice talk with the Bakers," the sheriff said.

Mr. Williams walked out into the front yard and down between the barn and the chicken yard. He was just noising around, trying to see how well the farm was being kept up. At the end of the corn rows, he could see the trees on the edge of the lake and decided to walk over and take a look. As he walked on closer to the trees, he could see the lake much better. He walked on as if something was leading him to somewhere. His steps took him to the spot where Alice had climbed onto dry land and challenged the snake. It was there that he looked down and saw a small boat still tied to a tree root. He smiled because he recognized the boat.

He started back to the house and met the sheriff who was coming to meet him.

"Have you seen anything interesting?" the sheriff asked.

"Not a thing," Mr. Williams walked on past the sheriff toward the car. "Thanks for the visit," he said to the Bakers as he passed them, getting into the car without hesitating.

The sheriff walked around to the other side of the car and got into the car and tooted a good-bye to the Bakers and drove off.

They drove down that dirt road without saying a word. When they passed the train station, the sheriff said, "Would you mind driving a bit, Mr. Williams. I'm a bit tired."

"Sure," Mr. Williams said and took the wheel. They got to the Williams's house at about four o'clock that afternoon. Before dropping Mr. Williams off, the sheriff said, "Now I feel good about closing that drowning case."

"Yeah," said Mr. Williams. "You can close it out now."

Mr. Robert Williams walked into the house, feeling very bad about raping Sarah and worst that his mother and wife knew that he had done it. He had no idea what he could do to make things better. His mother and wife had nothing to say to him, and every time Sarah looked at him, he could see the hate. Her hate may not have been so bad if she did not have to depend on his mother for her survival. Today, however, he is going to try to make things just a litter bit better. He went into the kitchen and sat at the table. "Sarah," he said. "Would you please ask my mother and wife if they would come to the table please?"

"Yes, sir," she said.

Sarah went into the sitting room and told Marge and Brenda, then out into the garden and told Mrs. Williams that they were wanted in the kitchen. Marge, who was in the sitting room waited for her mother-in-law because she did not want to face her husband alone. Mrs. Williams came into the house, washed her hands, and joined Marge in the sitting room, and then the two of them went into the kitchen and sat down at the table with Mr. Robert Williams. Mrs. Williams, the mother, was at the head of the table.

"Thank you all for coming," Mr. Williams told them as if he was calling a meeting in a business office. "First, I want to ask Sarah to forgive me for what I did to her. Then I want to ask my wife to forgive me for what that deed did to her. And Mama, I'm so sorry for the heartbreak that it has caused you to have to live with for the rest of your life.

"There is nothing that I can do to make this mess that I have created go away, but there is something that I can tell you that might help just a little bit. I have seen evidence that Josh is okay. This is very important to us, so please don't tell anyone that's not in this room." Then he told them about the boat at the edge of the lake.

After Mr. Williams had told the rest of the story, Sarah and his mother's tears ran down their cheeks. Marge looked in her husband's eyes and said thank you and went back into the sitting room.

Mr. Robert Williams left with a bit of relief, but his heart was still filled with fear that his story would get out. He left the house and headed for the bar. As he pulled out of his driveway, he met his daughter Brenda. She was walking back home from Grace's place. Her pregnancy was showing now and there were not so many friends around since she had stopped using the pool. Mr. Williams passed her as if he didn't see her. It was getting dark when he got to the bar and there were only a few clients there. As he walked into the bar, the bartender asked, "What do you have?

"Give me a Falstaff," Mr. Williams said and walked over to a table and sat down. He had a lot on his mind and was in a mood to be alone, so he sat there sipping his beer.

The sheriff walked in just as he was finishing his beer and said to the bartender, "Bring me the same as what Mr. Williams is having."

"I'll have another," said Mr. Williams.

"Two beers coming up," the bartender said.

It was then that Al and another one of David's friends came in and sat at their table,

"How is the investigation going?" Al asked the sheriff.

"I'm going to close the investigation," the sheriff said to Al.

Al said, "I'll bet you, David and old Brock ran into that Josh and that black girl and burst a cap in both of them." Then they started celebrating, drinking that corn liquor and fighting, and fell out of the boat. You know, neither one of them could swim worth a darn."

"Well, what do you think happened to the bodies of the two of them?" the sheriff asked.

"Alligators," Al said."

"Yeah, alligators," Mr. Williams said.

"I didn't expect to get too much information," said the sheriff. "I'm glad it's all over with."

CHAPTER 13

JOSH AND ALICE'S trip was mostly uneventful. It was the middle of March and Josh had expected the weather to be a little cold, but the wind was as cold as a ring around a polar bear's nose and it was blowing off Lake Michigan like a hurricane. It was nearly a whiteout and Josh had never seen anything like this before. The train was moving more slowly now because of the weather and Alice and Josh had no plans and no idea how big this city was or what they would do when they got to the train station.

There was one good thing that was in their favor, it was early in the morning and they had a full day to find somewhere to live.

When they stepped off the train, a porter picked up their bags and asked, "Where to, sir?"

Josh spoke up and said, "I need to find a place to stay. Can you help me?"

The porter looked at Josh and said with amazement, "Y'all come all the way from 'I don't know where' and you ain't got no place to stay?"

"That's right," Josh said. And we would surely thank you and my good God if you would give me some kind of idea where to start looking."

The porter said, "You got any money for cab?"

"Yes," Josh replied.

"Have a seat over there," the porter told them, pointing to a bench in the waiting room of the station. "I'll be with you after I finish with this train."

It took the porter a few minutes to finish with the other passengers then he came over to speak with Josh and Alice.

"I know a woman who runs a boarding house," he told Josh. "It doesn't cost too much, but you have to pay up front."

"We'll take anything for now," Josh said.

"Let me give her a call and see if she has any rooms," the man said.

"Thank you, sir," Josh said to the porter.

After a few minutes, the porter hung up the phone and said to Josh, "She has a room for you, my shift is over in about an hour and I live close to her place. Could I hitch a ride with you people to her place."

"Yes," Josh said. "I'd be glad to have you ride with us."

The boarding house was called Mary's Place and the ride there took about thirty minutes. Josh had time to ask Joseph, the porter, a lot of questions, such as where the unemployment office was and how to get to it.

Joseph the porter told Josh where the employment office was and how to get there. "The stockyard was just about always hiring, and it was a long ways out there but a person had a good chance of getting a job there."

"That's just what I need" Josh said. "A good chance for a job."

When they got to Mary's Place, the three of them got out of the cab. Josh paid the driver and followed Joseph into Mary's

Place. Joseph introduced Josh and Alice to Mary, the owner of Mary's Place. These are the people I told you about," Joseph added. "They need a room."

"It will be six dollars a week," Mary said, "starting now and at the beginning of every week thereafter."

Josh gave the woman six dollars. The woman shouted out. "Hey, Jean! Show these people to room twelve."

Jean, the woman who was working in the dining area, took them up to room twelve, showing them the community bath on their way up the stairway. Their room had a sofa, table with four chairs, and a pullout bed. The room was fourteen by fourteen with a kitchenette, and on the wall behind the table, a foldout ironing board.

As soon as Jean left the room and after figuring out how the foldout bed worked, Josh pulled the bed down and went to sleep on it while Alice slept on the sofa.

Josh had made plans to get up that next morning and go to the stockyard to try to get a job. When he woke up, Alice had been up for some time and had washed and ironed his best outfit and hung them over the radiator to dry. He looked at her and smiled, knowing that she was as tired as he was, yet she was up while he slept.

It was ten o'clock, he had gotten himself plenty of sleep so he pulled the information that he had gotten from Joseph out of his pocket and studied it, and then made plans on how he was to get to the stockyard that next morning. Joseph had said that the place opened up at eight. Josh's plan was to get there at seven. By six o'clock the next morning, Josh was up and ready to walk out of the house.

"You going out already, Josh?" Alice asked.

"Yeah," Josh answered.

"Did you put on your extra sweater? Now you be careful out there. It's mighty cold."

Josh closed the door and headed out into the cold dark Chicago morning. As he walked out of Mary's Place, he kept looking at his notes, take bus 166. The note read, "Take 166."

When he got on bus 166, the snow was falling much lighter than yesterday. The clouds were higher and lighter. *This is a good sign*, he thought. *Everything is going to be all right.*

After thirty minutes or so, he noticed that the bus was taking him out of the city. There were very few people on the bus now and the clouds were getting a little lower and the snow was getting a little thicker. *I hope I get there soon*, he thought. He tapped the man in front of him on his shoulder and asked him what time it was?

"It's six thirty-eight," the man said. "We are making good time."

"Are you going to the stockyard?" Josh asked the man.

"Yes," the man said. "I work there where they slaughter the animals."

"What do you do?" Josh asked.

"Cleaning and hulling the waste away," the man said." Are you looking for a job?"

"Yes, I am, and by the way, what is your name?" Josh asked.

"I'm Sam Brown," he said. "If you follow me, I'll take you to my boss. He may hire you right away if you don't mind hard, nasty work."

"I'll take anything," Josh said. "Take me to him."

Sam and Josh got off the bus at six forty-five. The temperature was about twenty degrees and the wind was still blowing the snow around. Sam took Josh to the gate and told the guard that he was taking Josh to his boss, Mr. Smith. They walked down this long hall that led to the slaughterhouse. When they got to the office, Sam knocked on the office door.

"Come in, Sam," Mr. Smith said.

Josh waited outside.

"I have a man out here who wants a job, and I think that he wants it bad or he would not be out here in this snowstorm."

Mr. Smith looked out the window at Josh. "Come in, young man," he said. He looked Josh over then asked. "What kind of work do you like to do?"

Josh said. "I'll do any job you have out here."

Sam brought you out here on a bad day. This place is close today because of the snowstorm," he said. Then he went to a file cabinet and pulled out some papers and gave them to Josh and said, "Fill these out and leave me your phone number."

"I don't have a phone number," Josh said.

Mr. Smith looked at Sam and said, "I'll call you when the weather clears up. You contact him," Mr. Smith told Sam.

"Yes, sir," Sam replied. The two men went back to the front of the building and waited there for the next bus. On their way home, Sam told Josh about the work that he would be doing and that he would call him on the phone at the desk in Mary's Place.

When Josh got back into their room, he found that Alice had cleaned up the place, folded the bed away, and she had gone out, purchased some food stuff, and stored it away in the cabinets.

On the table was a note that said, "I'm going out to see what I can find. See you when I get back."

When Alice came in that evening, she brought a heavier coat, pair of pants, and some underclothes for Josh.

He just smiled when he saw these items spread out on the table. *This is some woman*, he thought. Two days later, Josh got a call from Sam who said, "We have to go to work tomorrow and we need to take the six o'clock bus, and don't forget to put on some warm clothes, the hawk is going to be mean tomorrow morning."

"I know what you mean," said Josh, "and I'll be ready for the hawk."

The next day, he got on the bus, looked around, and saw his new friend Sam, sitting on the backseat. He went to the back where Sam was and sat beside him. "How are you doing?" he asked.

Sam said, "Fine, what about you?"

"I'm good," Josh told him.

"I see that you have got yourself a heavier coat. I thought you were going to freeze your butt off the other day," Sam said with a chuckle.

"I damn near did," Josh told him. "Do you think the man is going to hire me today?" Josh asked.

"You are already hired," said Sam. "It's going to be hard work but it will give you a start." Josh was filled with happiness when he heard that he had the job and thanked Sam for what he had done for him.

After a few days, Josh was starting to become relaxed in his work. He and Sam were becoming good friends, and Alice was waiting for a job to come through from any one of the many positions to which she had applied.

At the end of Josh's second week of work, he got his first check and took Alice out to a movie. When they returned to Mary's Place, some customers were having dinner at the diner. They commented on Josh and Alice being such a nice couple and someone asked how long they had been married.

Josh said, "We are not married." Without thinking of what the many middle-aged diners would be thinking.

The diners were shocked! The owner wanted them out that night. A minister, who was there that night, came over to them and told them that they were going straight to hell, then asked if they wanted him to pray for them.

Alice looked at Josh and asked, "Josh, will you marry me?"

Josh said yes then he turned to the minister and asked, "Sir, will you marry us here and now?"

Mary shouted out, "I'll be the witness."

"Me too," said someone in the far corner of the room.

"Do you really want to get married?" the minister asked.

The both of them said yes. And Josh added, "We have been thinking about it for some time now."

The minister married them and invited them to dinner at his table.

Mary brought over cake and wine. One visitor came over and toasted the couple and wished them luck. It was a very good day. All of the people laughed and sang joyful songs.

When Josh got Alice alone, he said, "I'm so glad that you asked me to marry you. It was just the right time and the right place. They were expecting a fight from us, but you cut it off at the bud," then he squeezed her tightly and said, "We were already married."

"Yes, we were," said Alice. "I will not love anyone but you." Then she looked deep into Josh's eyes as if she wanted to embed the words into his brains, she added, "I do love you very much and I always will."

The next week, the newlyweds had another bit of good luck, Alice was hired in the post office doing janitorial work. The night she got the job, she said, "We have got to get out of this room." Josh agreed with her and they started looking for an apartment the next week.

They picked an apartment midway between their two jobs and the bus stop was across the street from their apartment. Josh told Mary that they were going to move and thanked her for letting them move in with such short notice.

Mary smiled and said, "I knew that you were not going to stay here. You are not the type. I like you and your wife and would like to continue being friends with the both of you."

"I would like that too," Josh replied.

The apartment was a two-bedroom flat with a full bath and a kitchen with a refrigerator and stove. When Alice entered the place, she had smiles all over her face. She felt like a queen in her palace with her king and it wasn't long before there was a little prince, living in their palace with them.

In eight years, Josh had been promoted to the dispatch position and Alice had been moved over to the mail room. The little one, Joseph (named after the porter who helped them at the train station), was now seven years old. When Joseph started school, Josh and Alice had expected that he would be going to an integrated school, and his school was much better than the school that Josh and Alice had gone to, but in no way as good as the white schools across town.

Alice had been promoted to a new job of sorting mail and delivering it throughout the administrative section of the building. During her break, she would often sit at a table in the break room and have her coffee. Jeff, a young man from one of the offices that she had delivered some mail, saw her at the break room drinking coffee and came over to sit beside her.

"Do you mind?" he asked.

"No," she said. They chatted for a little while about the work that she did, but he never spoke of the work that he did. He later asked where she was from.

"I'm from a little place near Baton Rouge in Louisiana," she told him.

"Oh," he said, trying to impress her. "You are a country girl from the south."

"Yeah, I'm from the south. What about you?"

"I was born here," he said. "A pretty girl like you should be working in an office."

"I wish I could get a job in an office," she told him. Alice had hopes that this young man had some connections or may be able to introduce her to someone who could help her. They continued to chat for a few minutes then later that day, she asked her girlfriend about the young man.

"He's an office boy," her friend said. "What did he say to you?"

"He talked to me about getting an office job," Alice said.

"You have to watch out for that kind of guy," her girlfriend said. "He's lucky to have the job that he has and he's trying to impress you."

Jeff would make it his business to be wherever Alice would sit down to have a break. Then one day, he reached out to hold her hand. Alice knew what was going on but thought about what if. She drew her hand away but slowly. Her action, just the slowness of withdrawing her hand, encouraged Jeff. Afterward, his aggressiveness caused her to have second thoughts about their meetings.

The next day, she decided that she better have her coffee at her workplace. As she sat drinking her coffee, she thought of all the things that she and Josh had gone through together; how he had attacked a man in the creek; how they shelled corn, picked cotton, and nearly froze looking for a job. In her mind, there was no man that could come close to being a man like her Josh.

The next day, she took her break on a bench on the outside of the building. Jeff found her there sitting alone. He walked over to her and sat down beside her. "What are you doing here?" he asked.

"Drinking coffee," she said.

"We used to drink coffee together," he told her.

"From now on, I drink my coffee alone," she said, trying to give him a hint.

"I thought we were a couple," he said.

Alice could not hide the thoughts in her mind. She had thought of talking to him but later she thought better of it, thinking of how much she had to lose and decided to try and discourage him so she turned and looked at him, then she leaned back and spoke softly saying, "My husband is a man who has gone through some things that you have not dreamed of. He has been angry all of his life. I have to tell you that I don't want to get involved with you and you don't want to get involved with me, so if you see me sitting alone, it's because I want to be alone."

Jeff got up from the bench and went back to work, thinking of how harsh she had been and knowing that she did not want him around. Alice went home that evening thinking of what might have been and felt a little guilty because she had really thought seriously about it.

When she opened the door to her apartment, Josh was preparing dinner for the two of them. She rushed over to him and gave him a big hug, thinking, *What a foolish thought it was to think of cheating on a man like this.*

CHAPTER 14

BRENDA WAS GETTING ready to have her baby, the same time that Josh made that freezing trip to the stockyard to apply for his first job in the windy city. Her mother, Marge, thought it would be better that Brenda have the baby at the house. Grace was the only person, other than the family, who knew that Josh was the father of the infant, and all they had to do was to keep her quiet. It was Brenda's grandmother who had planned to encourage the doctor not to enter black on the birth certificate, and it was Brenda's job to make sure that Grace kept her mouth shut.

When Grace came to the house to be with her friend, Brenda asked her to keep it quiet about who the father of the baby was. Grace agreed and told her friend that she would keep it their secret.

Brenda's mother and grandmother assisted the doctor. When the baby arrived, Grandma stepped back and uttered, "Oh my god! The baby is dark and with some black features."

The doctor said "It's not white," and gave the baby to Marge. Marge took the baby, wrapped her in a blanket and gave it to Brenda. Mrs. Williams called the doctor out in the hall and had a talk with him.

It was a beautiful child and Brenda and her friend enjoyed having her around. After a few weeks had passed, Grace asked the most important question, "What school is she going to and how will her schoolmates treat her?"

"She's my baby," Brenda said, "and I'm white so why can't my baby go to a white school."

"You've got a lot to learn about this country," Grace said. "This white society cares only about the purity of itself, no matter how the mixture came about. The white group takes no blame for the mix, nor does it care about how small the contamination is. They will not accept her. They say that if a person has just one drop of black blood, that person is black; therefore, they would take those offspring, who are a mixture of both black and white and enslave them, even though they are their own descendants, according to their own rules. But this child will be accepted more readily in a black school than some of the black children."

"You mean that she will have to go to a black school," Brenda said.

"No one is going to completely accept her in the white society, not even her own family," Grace told Brenda.

Brenda turned to her friend Grace. She now understood what a mess that had been created because hate would not let love run free. She now knew why Josh, her brother, even though, he didn't know it, tried to keep her away from him. The tears swelled up in her eyes as she took little Betty in her arms and slowly walked back to her room.

Marge had only talked to Junior casually since she found out about him raping Sarah. Junior was out of the house most of the time, and he had not spent too much of his time checking on what was happening on the farm. The afternoon, when the doctor came to the house, Junior decided to spend some time down at the bar. The waitress, knowing how he loved his Falstaff, brought him one before he asked.

"Thank you," he said as he took his seat at the bar.

"Isn't it about time for your grandchild to arrive?" the waitress asked.

"It's due any day now," Mr. Williams said. Then he just sat there not saying a word.

"Is everything okay?"

He took a drink of his beer, got up from the bar and walked out, not saying a word.

Sarah, who had not seen the baby, went upstairs to Brenda's room. She took the baby into her arms and hugged it, saying, "She's such a sweet little girl."

"That's your granddaughter," Brenda said.

"I know," Sarah answered. It was the first of the many loving hugs that she would receive from her grandma Sarah.

Grandma Williams worked in her garden or sat in her room most of the day and Marge just went for long walks. Grace was forbidden to visit Brenda's house after her parents found out that the baby was black, which didn't take long after the baby was seen.

There were dark times in the Williams's house in those days. For a long time, there were no visitors because of the problems caused by incest, while the older Williams's women stayed in their separate rooms whenever they could. The tenants of the place were doing okay, but had a bit of trouble getting supplies. They knew that something was going on but they didn't know what it was until, while Sarah was taking care of the baby, Mrs. Jones came by to visit her.

Mr. Robert Williams had been drinking hard since the baby was born and Marge not talking to him didn't help. The guilt of raping Sarah lay heavily on his mind and he knew that all this mess in his house was caused by him. This was too much. He was easily agitated and got upset over little things. Williams had many conflicts with his tenants, and Grace's father, asked Mr. Robert to leave his bank because of his drinking. The combination of all of these things were just too much for Mr. Williams to bear.

Mr. Williams was found on the knoll by the creek with the gun in his hand and a bullet in his temple that following week. This tragedy brought more misery to the Williams's household than anyone could have ever expected.

There was much conversation about why he went to the knoll to kill himself. Was there a connection between him and the two men who had died there earlier, or was it a place where he had fond memories.

At the funeral, Mrs. Williams was devastated but hoped that this was the beginning of the end of the Williams's family tragedy. Sarah had kept Betty at her place while the three Williams women lay Mr. Robert Williams Jr. in his final resting place.

It was five years later when the three Williams' women talked with Sarah about Betty. They were looking for a solution to the problem of sending Betty to school. Grandma Williams pointed out that if Betty lived with Grandma Sarah, she would be officially black and go to the black school, and no one would consider putting her out.

The three of them agreed because Sarah was working in their house and they could see the baby any time they wished. They could take care of Betty's needs and Grandma Sarah would be her nanny.

Betty was a good student after entering school and was very happy with her peers. Mr. Smith was still the teacher, and the school had added two more rooms and two additional teachers. Sarah would take her to school each morning and bring her home every evening.

Brenda was ill and tired of hearing all of the gossip form the neighborhood so she talked her mother into taking care of Betty when Sarah was not around so that she could go to the Gulf Coast and stay with her grandfather for the summer.

CHAPTER 15

JOSH AND ALICE were doing very well taking care of themselves financially, but the cold weather was taking a great toll on Josh's health. It started in the tenth year on the job at the stockyard. At first, Josh started catching those nagging colds that he could not seem to get rid of. In the summer, he would get some relief but when the next winter came, the problem would get much worse. Josh's condition took quite a toll on Alice, but she hung in there with Josh and Joe and was never out of work.

It was late spring, Josh was on his way home from work. As he rode along the route from work to his apartment, he thought of his friend Jack. He had last seen Jack the evening before Jack left for Tuskegee, Alabama, and had often wondered where Jack was and how he was doing. At this point, his mind began to wonder, but his thoughts were mostly about his mother and visions of all of Swamp Town roamed about in his mind. It was at this time that a plan of how he was going to contact his mother was formulated.

When Josh got to his apartment, Alice was not home so Josh figured that she was working late. Because Alice was late, Josh started making preparation for the evening meal. This evening, they were having pork chops, stewed potatoes with onions, and string beans. Josh had just finished setting the table when he heard Alice's key at the door.

"Hello, Josh," Alice said as she walked through the door. "You've got it smelling good in here."

"Well, sit yourself down and enjoy it," Josh said. He then walked around to her side of the table and pulled her chair out for her.

"What's up?" she said with a bright smile on her face.

"Nothing," he said. "I just want to make you feel good." He was partly correct but the smirk on his face gave him away. "Well," he said as he sat down on his side of the table, "I do have something to discuss with you."

"What is it? she asked.

"On my way home today, I was thinking about Swamp Town and maybe trying to send Mama a message," then He added, "It's been ten years now, maybe no one is even looking for me."

"That may be okay, but be sure to go through Miss Jesse and tell her to talk only to your mother," Alice told Josh.

"Okay," Josh said." I'll be careful"

The next day, on his break, Josh sat down and composed a message to Jesse, telling her to tell his mother that he and Alice was all right, and they both were working then. In a P.S., he added that if she ever see Jack, give him his regards and say that if he was ever in Chicago, ask the porter at the train station for a place called Mary's Place. If and when he gets to Mary's place, ask for Mary and say that you are looking for a man named Josh. She can get in touch with me."

When Josh got home that evening, he showed the note to Alice and asked her what she thought of the message.

"I think that the message is just fine," Alice said. Then she added. "I'll mail it from the post office tomorrow with a no return address."

"Okay," Josh said.

The next day, Alice mailed the letter from the post office as she said she would do.

Jesse Mae had not received any mail in nearly five years. It was as if the postal service had forgotten that she was in Swamp Town. She was sitting at the bar that afternoon when the mailman walked in and handed her a letter. She was very excited, thinking that it was a letter from her son's father whom she had not heard from him in years, but there was no hope that he was sending any long forgotten child support money. She waited until the mailman left and there was no one else in the bar before she opened the letter.

"My Lord!" said Jesse Mae. "This is from Josh and Alice. I've got to tell Sarah as soon as I can." She went into the back room to lock the door, but when she came back to the bar, some customers had entered the place. She was smiling excitedly. The customers were pleased to see such a beautiful smile but had no idea that the smile was not for them. Now, she could not leave her customers, so she waited until she knew that Sarah had finished her work for the day.

Jesse Mae walked the three-quarter mile down the dirt road to Sarah's house. Sarah saw her coming up the path and waited for Jesse Mae at the front door.

"Go into the house," Jesse Mae said. When she got close enough for Sarah to hear. Sarah went into the house and left the door open for Jesse Mae to enter. Jesse Mae entered the house nearly screaming. "I've got some good news for you! I have a message from Josh and Alice, and they are all right."

Sarah sat down and allowed her tears to flow freely. Seeing the joy on Sarah's face brought the tears to Jesse Mae's eyes also. They sat there for a while, trying to compose themselves and enjoying the good news. Later, the two of them walked down the path to Alice's parents' house and the tears flowed again. Sarah spoke of the importance of not telling anyone else except Jack about the good news.

It was two months after Sarah had received her good news that Jack came to visit his parents. Jack did as he always did and stopped by to visit his friend Josh's mother, just to say hello. Jack had been feeling good about himself and had learned quite a lot about life and working on a job that had nothing to do with farming. His coworkers liked him and were glad to help him and he had been told that he would be trained to be a mechanic on airplane engines so he was home to tell the good news to all of his friends.

Jack had bought himself a new suit, white shirt, and black and white shoes. He was on his way to Miss Sarah's house to tell her how well he was doing. Before he got to the house, he took his handkerchief out of his pocket, dusted his shoes off, and then walked up on the porch and knocked at her door.

When Sarah opened the door, she was surprised to see such a well-dressed, handsome young man.

"Hello, Jack, how are you doing?" she asked.

"Hello," said Jack. "How are you doing, Miss Sarah? Have you heard anything from Josh?" he asked.

"Yes," she said. "As a matter of fact, I have. But you must keep it to yourself. Sit down," she told Jack. "Tell me what you've been doing."

Jack sat there for an hour, giving her all the details about the work that he was doing, his new friends that he had made, and what the place was like. Sarah listened quietly, while he told of his life in his new world.

When Sarah got a chance to get a word in, she said, "Josh told me to tell you that he would like to see you if you ever came to Chicago." She then wrote down the information that Josh had written about how he could make contact with him by asking the porter at the train station about Mary's Place and gave it to Jack.

Jack took the information, put it in his billfold and said good-bye to Miss Sarah.

Jack had been a hard worker since he came to Tuskegee and had taken very little time off, so his supervisor told him that he could start taking a week off every year to relax and enjoy himself.

"What am I going to do with a whole week off," Jack asked his supervisor. Jack had always thought of his trips to Swamp Town as being enough of a vacation. To him, his friends at work and his family in Swamp Town had been all the vacation that he had ever wanted but the thought of seeing Jack was very interesting.

The supervisor had suggested that he go on a trip and this gave Jack the idea. He would go to Chicago to see if he could find his friend, Josh. His supervisor had told him that he could take two weeks off, so he decided that he would do just that.

Jack was getting excited about seeing his best friend Josh. He wanted so badly to tell him what he had been doing, the new friends that he had made, but mostly he wanted to tell Josh that he had learned how to read.

Jack had saved his money penuriously by listening to Mr. Jacob, his mentor, who had taken him under his wing because he had shown such interest in his work. So for Tuskegee was the only place that Jack had ever been except Swamp Town and now he was making plans to travel to the big city of Chicago. It was Friday, the second of August, when Jack boarded the train heading to Chicago. He wore his black pinstripe suit, black and white shoes, and a black tie and had bought himself a new gray hat, but he was not used to wearing a hat so most of the time he kept the hat in his hand. The trip was long but uneventful. To him, it was just a long ride in the country.

He arrived at the train station in Chicago at ten thirty that Sunday morning. He got off the train, walked up the ramp, down the hallway, and into the biggest room that he had ever seen in his life. The noise was deafening and people were everywhere. He felt as if he was in another world.

A porter, who spotted Jack walking around as if he didn't know which way to go, walked up to him and asked, "May I help you, sir?"

"Yes, sir," Jack said. "I can use all of the help I can get."

"Where do you wish to go, sir?" the porter asked.

"I'm here to visit a friend. My friend told me that when I got here, I was to ask a porter about a place called Mary's Place. He said that when I got to Mary's Place, someone could tell me where I could find him." While the two of them were talking, another Porter walked up and spoke to Jack.

"How are you doing, sir? Can I help you?" the other porter asked.

The first porter said, "He's looking for a place called Mary's Place and says that a man called Josh told him that Mary could put him in contact with a man called Josh."

"Oh!" said the second porter. "I know Josh, and I know where Mary's Place is. Where are you staying?" asked the porter.

"Anywhere I can get a room," Jack told him.

"If you don't mind, I'll call Mary and see if she has a room available for you, then you can catch a cab to Mary's Place," the porter told Jack. When the porter returned, he told Jack that his room was ready. "I'll hail a cab for you to take over to Mary's Place and Mary will contact Josh for you," the porter told Jack.

.The porter went outside of the railroad station and hailed a cab for Jack, who arrived at Mary's Place at one thirty that Sunday afternoon. Mary met Jack at the door. "Hello," she said. "I'm Mary"

"I'm Jack," Jack answered. "I'm a friend of Josh."

"Are you staying with us, Jack? Mary asked.

"I hope to be staying for about five days."

"That will be two dollars a night." Mary called Jean and asked her to take Jack up to his room. "I'll call Josh and tell him that you are here," she said to Jack as he followed Jean upstairs to his room.

Josh was sitting on the balcony of his apartment when the phone rang. Alice, who was sitting in the living room, picked up the phone. "Who is it?" she asked.

"This is Mary down at Mary's Place," the voice said. "I have a visitor here for Josh."

"What is the name?" Alice asked.

"The name is Jack."

"Oh my god!" Alice yelled. "Josh! Josh!" she cried out! "Josh, Jack is here. He came to see you."

Josh jumped up from his chair, shaking in his voice and body. He wanted to scream but his voice came out barely audible. "Mama got the message, Mama got the message" was all he could say. By this time, Alice was out on the balcony with her arms around his neck.

"Where is Jack?" Josh asked.

"Oops!" Alice said. "I dropped the phone." She rushed back to the table and picked up the phone. "Hello! Hello, are you still there, Mary?"

"Yes," Mary said. "What happened to you?"

"Oh, I just got excited. I forgot to ask you where Jack was," Alice said.

"He's here at my place," Mary told Alice.

"Tell him, we'll be by to see him real soon." She hung up the phone.

"Let's get ready and go over to Mary's Place to see my buddy Jack," Josh told Alice. "It's been a long time."

"I'll be ready in a minute," Alice yelled from the bathroom. "I'm getting ready now."

Alice came out of the bathroom wearing a red short-sleeved blouse, a black knee-length skirt with a two-inch patent leather belt that was matching her patent leather white shoes. The smile on Josh's face gave her the approval that she was looking good.

They walked out of the apartment just as a cab was passing. Josh hailed the cab who had passed them but the driver went around the block and came back to pick them up. The driver got out of the cab and opened the door for the young couple so they could get in the cab and off they went to Mary's Place.

Josh was wearing khakis with a tan satin shirt. After about ten minutes on the way to meet Jack, Josh started coughing. It was not much, but he started to panic a bit, being careful not to get anything on his new satin shirt and he didn't want Jack to get the impression that he was ill. Alice told him that he should have the doctor to take a look at that cough and that it sounded like it may be something serious.

"I know! I know!" said Josh. "I'll be okay."

When they got to Mary's Place, Jack was waiting for them in the lobby. Josh and Alice rushed to their friend Jack and greeted him with warm hugs, then Josh called Mary over and asked if they could have a booth in the far corner so that they could talk and later have dinner. Mary agreed and told them to take their time.

As they sat down, Alice asked, "How have you been doing, Jack, and how are things at Tuskegee?"

Josh cut in and asked, "What about Swamp Town? Are they still looking for me?" Josh still had remnants of fear left from his flight out of Swamp Town.

"Not as far as I know," Jack said. "But you know how the clan is." Then he added, "They searched the creek and found two bodies. "Some say that those two men killed you, Josh, then they got drunk and killed each other fighting over Alice. I was scared that you were dead until I was told that the sheriff heard talk around town about you having been seen on a farm on the north side of Lake Pontchartrain. But when the sheriff returned to Swamp

Town, he said that he found no evidence there, so he closed out the case."

"What else is going on around Swamp Town," Josh asked.

"There is one thing, but I don't know if I should tell you," Jack told Josh.

"Tell me everything," Josh said." Tell me everything I need to know."

"It is about that relationship with you and Brenda at the creek," said Jack.

"What happened?" Josh wanted to know.

Something happened years ago between your mother and Mr. Williams that created the problem.

"What kind of problem?" Josh asked.

"I don't know how to tell you this, Josh. Jack wanted to tell Josh but he feared that it would break up their friendship" So after some hesitation, he uttered softly, "I beg you, Josh. Don't get angry with me. A man should not have to tell his friend what I have to tell you."

"Just tell me everything, Jack. Lay it on the line. I need to know it all."

Jack was hurt. He did not want to tell Josh the truth, but he was bound to find out sooner or later so Jack just let it out. "Mr. Williams raped your mother and you are his son, and that makes Brenda your sister. Furthermore, Brenda had your baby." Jack had spit it out all in one sentence. Then he added, "They say, because you and Brenda are half sister and brother, the baby is kinda slow and don't walk so straight. You know, Josh, because of that incest thing."

Josh put his head on the table. He had said that he wanted to hear everything, but he didn't need to hear it all, no not all of it at the same time. Alice heard the sound of his sorrow. She softly placed her hand on his shoulder, saying, "It's not your fault, Josh. It's not your fault."

Jack could feel Josh's pain, so he quickly changed the subject. "Josh, you know those people in Tuskegee where you and Mr. Smith sent me, they are some of the best people that I have ever met. They took me in, gave me a place to sleep, fed me and gave me a job. Mr. Jacob is still teaching me how to read and they are training me to work on airplane engines."

"How about that, Alice, they are teaching my buddy, Jack, how to work on airplanes." Josh placed his arm around Jack's shoulders, confirming what he had told Jack years ago—that he could do anything any man could do. All he needed was a chance.

"Did you find yourself a girlfriend yet?" Alice asked.

"There is someone that I'm talking to, but I don't know where it's going," said Jack.

Josh was feeling a little better about himself now. He sat up straight, raised his head, and said, "I'm really glad that those people are treating you so well, Jack." He hesitated, then asked, "Is she pretty?"

"Yeah," said Jack. "She is about Alice's height, a golden tan, very active and loves to go fishing."

Josh got a good chuckle out of that statement and said to himself, "He found someone as close to Alice as he could get."

Jean came over to the table and asked, "Are you folks ready to eat yet?"

"Yes," said Josh. "What's on the menu?"

"This evening, we are having our special which is chicken pastry, collard greens, fried sweet potatoes, and sweet tea," she told them.

"That sound like down home cooking," said Jack.

"It's close but it's from good old North Carolina," Jean said with pride.

"How did you know that dish was from North Carolina?" Josh asked.

"I was born in eastern North Carolina," Jean said, "in a little town called Bethel."

They all ordered the Carolina special. Afterward, the conversation changed to what they were going to do for the next three or four days. Jack had an invitation to go to church that Sunday with Jean. Josh and Alice had to work that Monday so Alice suggested that Josh take off that Wednesday and show Jack the town.

Monday was Jack's day to relax, so he did just that by taking a bus down town to see the city. The next afternoon, Josh stopped by Mary's Place and took Jack down to the neighborhood bar for a couple of beers. Josh was interested in how things were in Swamp Town and when was the last time he had been to Jesse Mae's place. While they were out, they talked about touring the city the following day.

Jack told Josh that Jesse Mae is still as sassy as she always was and she's still hitting on the young men. "I stopped by there a few days ago and talked with Miss Jesse and her son and they are doing just fine," he told Josh. "There are a few new people in the area but I don't know them."

"What did you say that your girlfriend's name was?" Josh asked.

"Lenora...Lenora Braxton."

"Where did you meet her?"

"One day, I was cutting grass on the east side of the airfield and saw her working in the field chopping cotton. I just walked over and started talking to her and we became friends."

"I hope you and Lenora lots of luck," Josh said. "You deserve it." Josh took Jack for a ride around town to see some sites then dropped him off at Mary's Place. That Thursday morning, Jack took the train back to Swamp Town.

CHAPTER 16

JOSH AND ALICE had been in Chicago for ten years and Josh's cough had not gotten any better. Alice was getting a bit concerned about his condition and insisted that he go see a doctor, but Josh had never agreed to go and see the doctor; however, this day, he went with Alice to see her doctor, a woman who had been treating her since she gave birth to her son.

This day, when Josh accompanied Alice to see Dr. Mary Warren, when they entered the treatment room, Alice told Dr. Warren that Josh was there to see her about a cough that he had had for a long time.

"So you finally got Josh to come in and let me take a look at him," said Dr. Warren.

Josh was shocked but tried not to show it. "I came in with her," Josh said with a pleasant voice. "I didn't know that she was bringing me in to see you"

Alice had feared that Josh would be angry that she had brought him in to see the doctor without him knowing it, but he did not seem angry and that pleased her.

"How long have you had this cough?" the doctor asked Josh.

"About four or five years," said Josh.

"Does your chest feel congested?"

"Yes, and it seems to be getting worse."

"We are going to have to run some test."

When the doctor came out of the room with Josh, Alice asked, "How is he doing?" Wanting to know what was going on with Josh.

"We want know until we take a look at the test results," the doctor told Alice. "I'm going to send you downtown to have some tests done. When I get the results back, I'll have you come in, then we will have a talk about your condition," she told Josh. "Have a seat for a minute. The clerk will make an appointment for you."

When they left the doctor's office, they walked quietly on the way to the bus stop. When they got to their seats in the bus, Alice sat near the window. She stared out the window and said without looking at him, "I'm sorry, Josh."

"For what?" Josh asked.

"For bringing you to see the doctor without you knowing it," she said.

"Oh, that's all right. I needed to come to see her."

"Well, I hope that they find out what is wrong and get you well again."

"I'll be all right," he said. "I'll be all right."

When they got back to their apartment, Josh sat on the sofa with a worried look on his face. He had never been really sick before. He wanted to talk to Alice but had no idea what to say to her, so he just sat there.

Alice went to the bedroom, trying to find some work to do so she decided to go to the laundrymat and wash some cloths. Josh she called from the bedroom, "Are you going to be here when Joseph gets home from school?"

"I'll be here." Josh answered.

"I'm going to the Laundromat to wash some clothes," she said. "I'll be back soon."

"Okay, babe, I'll be right here when he gets home."

Alice gathered the dirty clothes and headed off to the Laundromat.

Joseph was now eight years old and doing very well in school. The bus dropped him off a block from his apartment, making it easy for him and his three friends to walk together to their homes. When Joseph arrived at the door, Josh was waiting for him.

"Hey, Joe, How did it go today?" Josh asked.

"Okay," said Joseph as he rushed across the room, flinging his book bag on the sofa where Josh was sitting. Joseph was a healthy young man with the complexion of his mother and the light eyes and hair of his father. He enjoyed his school and friends on the south side of Chicago. This was his home and everyone treated him like the homeboy he was.

"Where is Mama?" Joe asked his father (Joe was what his mother called him).

"She went to the Laundromat," his father told him.

"Can I have some orange juice?" Joseph asked.

"Be careful and don't spill anything," Josh told him. "By the way, do you have any homework?"

"Yeah, a little math."

"Well, work on that when you finish your orange juice."

"Okay, I will."

When Alice returned with her washed cloths, Josh was still sitting on the sofa and Joseph was at the kitchen table doing his homework. She walked in with the basket of laundry under her arms, saying, "Joe, have you finished your homework?"

"Yeah, Mom, I'm just finishing up," said Joseph.

"Did you talk to the teacher about being in that play that you told me about?" Alice asked.

"Yeah, Mom. I'm going to play the part of the mailman."

"I'll be glad to see you up there on that stage, honey." Alice turned to Josh and asked, "How are you doing this afternoon?"

"I'm okay," Josh said, "but I don't want to talk about my situation until we get the report from the doctor."

"Okay," said Alice. "We'll wait until then."

Brenda had just returned from Baton Rouge with some clothes that she had just purchased for Betty. Betty had lived at Sarah's place for some time now and she seemed to be more at home there than at her Grandma Williams's house and Brenda liked it that way. Sarah loved her grandchild and took very good care of her and this was good for Grandma Williams, too, because she could see her granddaughter anytime she wished.

As Brenda approached Sarah's place, Betty noticed her mother coming to see her and she jumped off the porch and ran to meet her mother who put her packages under her left arm, took her daughter with her right hand, and walked her back to Sarah's porch where Sarah stood waiting.

"Hey, Sarah," said Brenda. "How have you and my little girl been doing?"

"We are doing just fine," said Sarah. "What about you?"

"I'm okay. I bought some things for my little girl," Brenda told her.

The three of them walked into the house and sat down with Betty cuddling as close to her mother as possible. Brenda started to open some of her packages, while all the time, saying, "Guess what Mama got her little girl."

Betty and Grandma Sarah marveled at all of the beautiful things that Brenda had bought for Betty.

"These things are all so pretty," said Sarah. She lay them out on the bed, matching the colors together. Sarah was smiling with the biggest smile, knowing how much Brenda loved her child. She was so happy that they had asked her to take care of Betty.

Brenda was quiet now. She sat there, saying nothing for a long time while Betty and Grandma were happily trying on her clothes. Sarah was starting to wonder, what was on her mind? What was bothering her? Sarah got up and walked over and sat beside Brenda and asked, "What on your mind, honey?"

"I was just wondering what ever happened to Josh," she said. "I wonder what if he didn't get hurt? You know, they never found any evidence that he was ever in the creek and Daddy said that he had seen evidence that Josh might not be dead. What do you think, Miss Sarah?"

"I just hope that wherever he is, he is all right," Sarah answered.

"If you get any news of him, Miss Sarah, will you please let my Grandma know?" She worries so much about him.

"I will," said Sarah.

"Now, my little girl and I are going for a walk." She took Betty's hand and asked her if she would like to go and visit her other grandma.

When they walked away, Sarah sat in her rocking chair on her front porch and wondered if she should have told Brenda that she had heard from Josh.

When Brenda got home, Grandma Williams, who had been a bit ill for the last few days, was still in her bedroom finishing her breakfast that Marge had brought her. Before Brenda and Betty got to Grandma's bedroom door, Betty pulled away and rushed into Grandma's room, saying, "Look, Grandma! Look what Mama got me, and I've got some more things in this bag," she said.

"Come here," said Grandma. "Come here and let Grandma see your pretty clothes."

Brenda came into Grandma's room and placed the clothes on the bed for Grandma to see then she sat down on the bed beside her grandma and said, "I had a little talk with Sarah today."

"What did you two talk about?" Grandma inquired.

"I asked her if she had heard from Josh."

"And what did she say?"

"Nothing really. Just that if he was alive, she hope that he was all right," Brenda told her.

"I hope that he is all right, too," said Mrs. Williams.

Just then Marge walked through the doorway and asked, "Did I hear someone speak Josh's name?"

"Yes," said Brenda, "But no one knows where he is or if he is alive."

"I hope that he is alive," said Marge. "He didn't do anything wrong."

"I hope that he comes home too," said Mrs. Williams. "He is my first grandchild."

Two weeks had passed since Josh had visited the doctor. His cough had gotten a bit worse so he had decided to take that Friday afternoon off. When he got home, he checked his mail as he always did and found that there was a letter from Dr. Mary Warren addressed to him. Alice was not home so he decided to wait until she got home so that they could read the good or bad news together.

When Joseph got home that afternoon, Josh was sitting there on the sofa with the letter in his hand. Joseph could tell that something was wrong because his father did not even speak to him.

"What's wrong, Dad?" Joseph asked.

"Nothing important, I just have to talk to your mother about something," he told his son. "You go into the kitchen and eat your snack then get to work on your school assignment."

"Okay," Joseph said. "But I don't have much to do." Joseph went to the kitchen, made himself a peanut butter sandwich, and got himself a glass of milk then went to work on his school project.

Josh just sat there. Normally, he would have been cooking the evening meal for the three of them, but this evening, he would wait for Alice to come home. Alice was feeling good that evening and decided to stop by the shoe store and purchase herself a new pair of shoes. She was only a few minutes late getting home but to Josh it seemed like hours. Josh was still sitting on the sofa with the letter in his hand when Alice walked through the doorway.

"Hi, honey, how was your day?" Alice said as she entered the room.

"I'm okay," said Josh. "Just a little upset about this letter."

"What letter?" asked Alice.

"I came home early today because I was having a coughing spell. When I got here, I checked the mail and found this letter in the mailbox," he told her. Then he handed her the letter. She took the letter, read who it was from, and dropped her arms to her sides, walked over and sat down on the sofa beside him. She let out a deep breath. "It's from Dr. Warren," she said softly.

"Yeah," said Josh. "Open it and read it."

The letter read that Josh has an appointment next Monday the 23 at two forty-five.

"I wonder what was wrong," Alice said.

"The letter just said that she wanted to see me on the twenty-three of the month."

"What does she want to see us about? I wonder," said Alice. She was talking to herself more than she was talking to Josh. Her worrying was beginning to get on Josh's nerve, but he dared not say anything because he too wondered what the problem was.

"We only have to wait a week," Josh told her. "We can wait that long. Now, what do you want for dinner?" he asked her.

"What about some fish cakes, rice, and cabbage?" Alice ordered.

"Coming right up," said Josh.

Alice went home.

Josh had seen the doctor and had gotten the bad news.

"What do you think of the doctor's instructions?" Alice asked Josh.

"Do you mean about going back down south? he asked.

"Yes," said Alice. "She thinks you should move down south and try living in the warmer climate. It might help you," she told him.

"What about our troubles in Swamp Town?" Josh asked.

"There may not be any trouble in Swamp Town," she told Josh. Then she hesitated before looking into Josh's eyes and saying, "What if I went to Swamp Town and see what I could find out."

"Why would you want to do that?" Josh inquired.

Alice spoke with a soft voice and said, "I want to see my mama." Then looking at Josh, she said, "I want my mother to see her grandson."

Even though Josh had never seen his wife complain, he knew that she loved her parents and wanted to see them. He had felt her pain in the past, but now that he had heard her say it and seen the look in her face, it broke his heart. He also wondered how it would be if he could see his mother, to walk the dirt road down to Jesse's place. He would give this some thought and hoped that it would be good for his health.

Alice had been taking time off one day at a time, but she had never had a two-week vacation, so she surprised her supervisor and asked for two weeks off.

"When do you want that time off?" her supervisor asked.

Alice knew that she wanted and needed the time off, but she had never spoken to Josh about when or how she was going to get to Swamp Town, so she said to her supervisor that she would tell him in a day or two. On her way home, she concentrated on her dilemma. She tried everything that she could think of to tell Josh how badly she wanted to see her parents, not to mention how much she hoped the warm weather might help him.

When Alice got home that evening, Josh opened the door and asked Alice, "When are you going to make plans for your trip to Swamp Town."

"Josh, You must have been reading my mind, I' have been thinking about that all afternoon," she told him.

Josh suggested that she take some money from the savings account and add it to her check and use that for her trip."

"I want to take Joseph with me," she said.

"I thought that was why you were going to see your mother," Josh said.

"Yeah, I know," she said. "I just want to make sure that we understand each other."

"Understood," said Josh.

The next day, Alice went into her supervisor's office and told him that she wanted the following two weeks off. It was that Tuesday of the week before Alice was to leave on her visit to Swamp Town, so she had a few days to prepare for the trip. It had been so long since she had seen her parents. She wondered how her father felt about her leaving without telling him, how she had kept his first grandson from him for so long. She was sure that her mother's love was still there, but her father, she feared that he would hate her and that made her nervous.

The rest of that week, she spent buying clothes for herself and her son, then she got all the things that Josh would need but had not thought of on that Friday evening, including gifts for her parents and Sarah.

That Saturday morning, Josh called a cab for Alice and their son Joseph and rode to the train station with them. This was the first time that Joseph had ever been out of the big city of Chicago. Alice was both nervous and excited and Josh was just lonely but he wanted them to go to see her parents.

They stood on the platform, waiting for their transportation to arrive. Joseph had no idea of what he was about to see. The great crowds grew larger and larger, getting closer and closer to the platform's edge, then there was a whistling sound coming from the right and every head turned to see what was coming. When Joseph saw it, he had an awe-inspiring feeling. It was a huge black monstrous machine with bellows of smoke rushing from its smoke stack and as it came to a stop, there were great amounts of steam being ejected from a pressurized steam valve causing a sound like he had never heard before. He stood there watching a great number of people getting off this train. After a few minutes, he heard a man yell, "All aboard! All aboard!"

The train left Chicago at 6:05 that Saturday morning. As they entered the train, Alice could see that Joseph was excited and was beginning to learn that the world was a lot more that what he had seen on the city streets. It was a clear, beautiful day and Joseph had sat by the window so he could look out and see. After crossing the city limits, Joseph could see the world spread out before him, At first, what he saw was a lot of nothing but as they rode along, his mother pointed out things that he never thought much about, like what his food looked like before it got to the table. There were fields of corn, fields of wheat, and herds of cows. Alice spoke to him about how those things got to his table, and about where his hamburgers and fried chicken came from. She even surprised herself about the things that he did not know, that she could tell him, and he had plenty of questions.

Alice and Joseph spent most of the night sleeping and were awakened by the porter the next morning, saying that the next stop was Baton Rouge. Alice and her son gathered their things and walked out of the station to a waiting cab.

The driver asked, "Do you need a cab, lady?"

"Yes," said Alice.

The driver got out of the cab and put her belonging in the trunk of the car. He opened the door of the cab for his passengers and asked, "Where to, Lady?"

"Swamp Town," said Alice.

The trip to Swamp Town was about ten miles with the last four miles on a dirt road, following the creek toward Lake Pontchartrain. It was about seven thirty that Sunday morning, the fog was thick all along the edge of the creek and there were no humans to be seen the last five miles to Swamp Town. Joseph's mind was in search of information but there was very little to be had, somewhere along the way, he asked, "Where are the people?"

Alice said, "We are just about home now. You'll see your grandparents soon." Five minutes later, the cab pulled into Alice's parents' yard. While Alice was paying the driver, Joseph had gotten out of the cab and was looking around taking in all of the new sights that he had never seen before. By the time Alice got out of the cab, her mother was standing in the doorway screaming, "Jake! Jake! Come to the door." Then she just stood there, holding her hands, while tears of joy ran down her cheeks.

Jake was a religious man but his church did not have service every Sunday, so on Sundays when there was no church, he would spend some time reading the Bible. This Sunday, that is what he was doing when he heard his wife's call. He promptly got up from the table and went to the front door to see what his wife wanted. When he got to the door, his daughter was rushing to her mother with open arms. When Joseph saw this, he rushed to his mother and grandmother and hung on to the both of them.

Alice's father just stood there, watching his wife, daughter, and grandson love each other. When Alice saw the smile and tears on his face, she knew that all was forgiven. Mr. Wilson reached out his open arms and welcomed his daughter. Joseph followed his mother over to his new grandfather. When Mr. Wilson saw the look of love and peace in their eyes, he knew that all was well.

For the rest of that day, Alice took her son around her old home site. They went to visit the animals. She spoke of how she used to feed them and how it was her job to milk the cows. She pointed to a place where Josh used to go fishing and told him,

"That's where your father did a lot of fishing. I'll take you there before we go back home."

Alice was a bit tired and decided to take a little break before she went visiting. After Alice took a nice long nap, when she got up, she went to the kitchen where her mother was cooking the Sunday meal. This Sunday, she was having chicken pastry, turnip greens, and corn bread with molasses pudding. The aroma in the kitchen brought back the memories of her childhood and just as she sat down, Joseph walked in and asked, "What's smelling so good?"

"That's the smell of Grandma's good cooking," Alice told him.

"What are you cooking," Joseph asked his grandma.

"Some chicken pastry, your mother's favorite meal and a molasses pudding," Grandma told him.

"It smells real good," Joseph said.

"Hope you like it," said Grandma.

"What do you have planned for tomorrow?" Mrs. Wilson asked her daughter.

"I want to take Joseph to see his other grandma," said Alice.

"She'll probably be working," her mother said. "But I think that it will be all right to speak to her in the kitchen."

Joseph should be able to meet his whole family," said Alice's father, who had overheard the conversation. He walked into the room where the ladies were talking and asked, "Why don't you take him over to see his other grandma now? It's Sunday evening and she's sure to be home."

"I think that I will do just that," said Alice. She called Joseph, who was sitting on the front porch. "Come here," she told him. "Put some clean clothes on. We are going over to your other grandma's house and talk with her for a while." Joseph dressed in his new grey short pants, white short-sleeved shirt, and new black shoes.

After Joseph was dressed, he called out to his mother, "Come on, Ma, I'm ready."

"Okay," his Mother said. "I'll be right there."

Joseph and his mother headed down the dusty dirt road to his other grandma's house. The walk to grandma Sarah's place was a little over a quarter of a mile. When they got within a few feet of the porch, Alice said. "Hold up a minute, Joe." She reached into her purse, pulled out a paper tower and cleaned of Joseph's new shoes. Then they walked to the door and knocked.

Sarah had been relaxing at home, resting, and getting ready for a new week of hard work that would come to soon. She was still in pretty good health, but the tiredness seemed to catch up to her a bit earlier each week as time went by. As Sarah approached the door, she couldn't help but wonder who could be visiting her this Sunday evening. "Who is it?" she asked.

"It's me, Miss Sarah, I've got someone who would like to see you."

Sarah didn't know who it was but she opened the door anyway. Her face lit up when she saw that it was Alice with her son Joseph. "Who is this young man?" she asked.

"This is the one who would like to see you," said Alice.

Sarah, moved out onto the porch, then closer toward Joseph, when her eyes met his. She said, "My Lord! OH, MY LORD! This is Josh's boy. Come on in! Come in. Tell me everything. Is Josh here? Where is Josh?"

Alice went inside and set down on the sofa and relaxed with a sigh of relief. Then she said, "Josh is not here but he is doing just fine; however, I wanted Joseph to see his two grandparents and get to know them."

Alice hesitated for a minute, trying to ease into a conversation about Josh and the doctor's suggestion that he try to get away from such cold weather.

When she had relaxed a bit, she said, "Josh works at the slaughterhouse, just outside of the city of Chicago and because of the conditions there, it has caused him some medical problems. The doctor has suggested that he would be better off if he move back to a warmer climate. The doctor thinks that the warm weather will be better for his health."

"What is he planning to do?" asked Sarah.

"The other reason I came down here is to see if Josh is in any real trouble," she told Sarah.

"I don't think he is, but we can get more and better information from the Williamses," Sarah replied. "I do know one thing," Sarah added. "Mrs. Williams wants him back home and Brenda never accused him of anything."

"Do you think that I should take Joseph to see the Williams?" asked Alice.

"Yes! Yes!" said Sarah. "I believe that she will be happy to see him."

"Will you come with us?" Alice asked.

"Of course, I will. I would be glad to," said Sarah. "Just let me get some clothes on."

After putting her clothes on, Sarah came to her bedroom door and said, "Marge is probably in the kitchen. Come on," she said to Joseph, "let's go visit some more of your people."

They walked out of the door and walked a couple of hundred yards to the big house. Sarah went to the kitchen door as if she was going to work, but this time, she had some very important people with her.

Marge had taken it upon herself to prepare a good Sunday meal for her mother-in-law in addition to taking on part of the duties that her husband had been doing. When she heard the knock at the back door, she wondered what had gone wrong. Did one of the tenants have an emergency, or maybe something was wrong with Sarah. When Marge opened the door, there stood Sarah with two other people.

"Hello," said Sarah. "I have some people that you and Mrs. Williams might want to see."

"Hello," said Marge. "Come into the parlor and have a seat. I'll get the Williams." Marge went to the stairway and said,

"Brenda, come to the door for a minute." When Brenda came to the door and looked down at Marge, Marge said, "Go and tell your grandma to come here, there is someone special to see her."

Brenda brought Betty downstairs with her and went to her grandma's bedroom and said, "Grandma, you have some special company."

In a few minutes, all four of the Williamses entered the parlor. Marge spoke first, asking Sarah to introduce the visitors.

Sarah said, "Mrs. Williams, this young lady is Alice, the daughter of Mr. Jake Wilson and this young man is her son Joseph, the son of Josh."

Mrs. Williams sat on the sofa and wiped a tear from her eyes. "Come here young man, let me have a look at you," she told Joseph.

Joseph walker over and stood close to where Mrs. Williams sat.

"I can see that it really is Josh's son. I can see it in his eyes," Mrs. Williams said. "Where is my Josh?"

Sarah was surprised that Mrs. Williams had called Josh her son and she was also pleased. To Sarah, this meant that Mrs. Williams loved her grandson.

Alice spoke up saying Josh is home. He and I are married.

"Congratulations," said Mrs. Williams and Marge.

Brenda walked over to Alice and gave her a hug and said, "I wish you and Josh happiness for the rest of your life."

"Thank you," said Alice. "I'm glad you feel that way."

"Sarah told Mrs. Williams that Alice had brought her son to see his family and I think that she may have something to tell you about Josh."

"What is it, Alice? What do you have to tell me."

"Well," said Alice, "Josh has been working at the stockyard in all of that cold, damp weather and has been coughing for the last three years. I took him to the doctor and the doctor says that he has pneumonia that's probably caused by exposure to the cold and/or the chemicals used in cleaning the place. The doctor thinks that he may be helped if he moves to a warmer climate and get away from those chemicals. I'm here to see if there will be any trouble if we move back to this area.

"I don't think so," said Brenda.

"Of course not," Mrs. Williams replied. "I'll see to that." The case has been closed for years and I'm going by the courthouse tomorrow and check for myself."

"There was only one person who had a problem with Josh and he died in that accident," said Marge.

"It would be good to have Josh back around this place. Let's pray that he gets well and comes back to us," said Mrs. Williams. "I'll be so happy to see him back here where he belongs.

"Come to the kitchen," said Marge. "I have a pot of coffee on, let's sit and talk. Alice can tell me all about where she has been."

The rest of the afternoon, the four ladies spent their time in casual conversation. It was amazing how much they learned about each other by sitting and having a little cup of coffee. When it was all over, Mrs. Williams asked Alice to meet with her for the trip to the courthouse that Monday morning.

Alice reported to the Williams house at eight thirty as she said that she would and went to the front porch to wait for Mrs. Williams. Mrs. Williams came out of the house promptly and the two of them drove off to Baton Rouge. At the courthouse, Mrs. Williams and Alice walked into the record section and asked the clerk for the information on the drownings of the two men in the creek on the date in question. The clerk searched the record and printed out a copy for Mrs. Williams.

On their way out of the courthouse, Mrs. Williams gave the copy of the information to Alice. "This is for you," she said. "I already know what it says. I checked it years ago."

"Thanks," Alice said. "Thanks for everything that you are doing for me."

"It's not for you," she hesitated for a few seconds, and then said, "My daughter-in-law, it's for me. I love Josh. I always did.

I was the reason that he didn't know that Brenda was his sister. When you see him, tell him that I want him home."

Alice could feel a tear in her eye, but she could not stop it nor could she stop the smiles that covered her entire face. When they got back to the house, Alice went into the kitchen to speak to Sarah. Mrs. Williams stopped in the parlor and spoke with Marge and Brenda. "I want Josh back here with me," she said. "He is my flesh and blood, and I need a man to manage this farm." Mrs. Williams then turned to Marge and said, "I want to thank you for taking care of the business part of the farm, but now I need someone who can go out in the field and make sure that the work is being done correctly."

"I'm okay with that," said Marge. "I've been thinking about going back to the coast."

"Me too," said Brenda, who had recently completed her degree in elementary education and had been offered a job in Baton Rouge. "I've been thinking about getting me an apartment in Baton Rouge when I start work, but I'll be in and out often to see you and Betty, Grandma."

"You had better," said Grandma. "I do want you all around me as much as possible. Let's just hope that Josh is okay and can come home soon."

"Where is Joseph?" Alice asked when she entered the kitchen.

"He and Betty said that they were going to set on the front porch just as you came in," said Sarah.

Alice walked around to the front porch where Joseph and Betty were sitting and called him, saying, "Let's go to Grandpa Wilson's house and see how they are doing."

Alice felt good walking back to her father's house. Joseph was wearing his shoes, kicking up the sand and dirt as he walked back to his grandpa's place. They walked past the house because they saw Grandpa at the barn. Alice's mind drifted back to the time when she helped Josh slip away from a dangerous situation. That was a long time ago and she often wondered what would have happen if they had gotten caught.

"Hey, Grandpa, What are you doing?" Joseph inquired.

"I'm feeding the animals," his Grandpa said. "You want to help?"

"I'll pitch some hay down, Joe. You help Grandpa put it in the trough," said Alice and up the ladder, Alice went as she had done many times before. She pitched the hay down while Grandpa and Grandson fed the animals. As she watched them work, she couldn't help but feel that the family would be getting back together. Joseph was watching all the animals and equipment that he saw on the farm with amazement and there was happiness in his face.

At supper time, the family had a long talk about what they were planning. "If Josh agrees to come back here, when do you think it will happen?" Mr. Wilson asked.

"It's hard to tell," said Alice. "We'll have so much to do." Alice gave him the papers that Mrs. Williams had given to her. The papers stated that the two men in question had drowned accidentally with no mention of Josh.

The next day, Alice decided to visit some of her friends. When she left the house, she had plans to visit the Jones's place, but when she and Joseph got there, she found that there was no one at home so she turned around and walked in the other direction. When they got near Grandpa's house, Joe, who seemed to enjoy walking in the sand and kicking up the dust said, "Let's go for a walk in that direction," pointing past Grandpa's house.

"Okay," said Alice, "but it's a long way down there." Seeing Joe walking down the dirt road was reminiscence of the times that she had walked the same road with his father. "Come on, Joe. Let's see who can walk the fastest." The faster she walked, the harder it was for Joe to keep up. Alice could feel great joy, walking and playing with her son the same way that she had played with his father. "If you catch me, I'll buy you a cold drink when we get to that store," she said to Joe, pointing at Jesse Mae's place.

Joe started walking faster and faster while Alice slowed down just enough for him to catch her just as she entered Jesse Mae's place. "You got me," she said to Joe. "I guess I'll have to buy you a cold drink." When they entered the store, Joe walked over to the counter and said, "Give me an orange crust, and she's paying for it."

A young lady who was working behind the counter asked Alice, "What will you have?"

"Give me the same," said Alice and then she asked, "Is Jesse Mae here?"

"Yes," said the clerk. "She's in the back room."

"Tell her that someone wants to see her."

"Miss Jesse," the clerk called out, "someone's here to see you."

"I'll be right there," Miss Jesse said.

Miss Jesse took the time to finish what she was doing and removed her apron before she came into the room. "Who wants to see Miss Jesse?" she asked.

"One of your best friends," said Alice.

Jesse Mae came to the bar and asked, "Who is my best friend? I want to see this person."

"I'm over here," said Alice, who was sitting in her usual seat with her son.

"Is that you?" Jesse Mae said. As she approached the two people who were sitting at the table in the corner of the room, she stopped again. "That is you! It's Alice! Where have you been, young lady, and who is that with you?"

"This is my son, Joseph. I brought him down here to see his family," Alice told Miss Jesse Mae. Then Alice turned to Joe and said, "This is Josh's son."

"You don't have to tell me," Miss Jesse Mae said. "I can see it in his eyes. By the way, where is Josh?"

"He's up north, you know. It takes a lot of money for three people to travel on a train."

"Yeah, I know," said Miss Jesse Mae. She also understood that Alice didn't want to tell her exactly where Josh was. She could wait. Miss Jessie Mae said to herself, "She is my best friend."

Alice got up from the table and asked Joseph if he was ready to go then turned to Miss Jesse Mae and said, "We'll talk more later." That satisfied Miss Jesse Mae, now she knew that there was more to the story. When Alice walked out of the door, she turned and said, "It's been nice talking with you.

The following day was the day before Alice and Joe was to leave to go back to Chicago. She had made plans to go by and see Sarah and the Williamses so she got up that morning and had breakfast with her parents before her father went to work.

Since she had to leave early the next morning, she would have a word with Sarah in the kitchen and hope to have a few words with the Williamses. When she got to the kitchen, the Williamses were just finishing their breakfast. Mrs. Williams invited Alice and Joe in for coffee.

"Are you getting ready to leave today?" asked Marge.

"No," said Alice. "We'll be leaving early tomorrow morning. We just came over to say good-bye and to say that we hope to see you again soon."

"I may not be here when you get back," said Brenda. "Good luck to you and yours."

"Thank you," said Alice. "And good luck to you in your teaching career."

Joseph had walked over, pulled up a seat, and sat down close to Betty. She smiled at him and asked, "Are you hungry?"

"Nope," said Joe.

All of those who were there could see the beginnings of a friendship between the two siblings. This day was the last day of Alice's trip to Swamp Town to check out the neighborhood to see if it would be safe for Josh to return. All was looking well and

Alice had decided to rest up for that long ride back to Chicago the next day. She was home with her mother and Joe had gone out with his grandpa to explore the area.

Grandpa had taken Joe to the creek, then into the wooded area. "Be quiet here," he told Joe. "You may see something that you have never seen before and we should keep a sharp eye out for snakes." They sat there quietly and Joe's first surprise was a sleeping owl. Next, he saw two huge frogs sitting around as if they owned the place. Then Grandpa touched Joe on his shoulder and said, "Look to your right, on the ground, about fifteen feet away."

Joe searched the ground for a few seconds and then said quietly, "That's a snake. Grandpa, that's a snake."

"Yeah," said Grandpa. "It's a dangerous snake. It's called a water moccasin, beware of him." The snake moved away and around a cypress tree trunk, then down into the creek. Grandpa took his grandson a little further along the edge of the creek where he was growing a field of rice. There, Joe saw some egrets and swans wading in the flooded fields. When they started back toward the creek, Joe encountered a huge spider web which looked like strings of gold. Joe was amazed. "The web look like strings of gold," he said to his grandpa. "I have never seen anything like this before. What is this?"

"It's the web of a large spider," his grandpa said. "For some reason, his web does look like strings of gold."

"I never saw a spider web like that before," said Joe.

"This is the only place that I've seen them," his Grandpa said. "Have you ever been fishing?"

"No," said Joe.

"Well. If you come back to visit me again, I'll take you fishing." His Grandpa promised him.

"That will be just great," said Joe.

"Let's go back to the house now, Joe. I'm getting a little hungry."

"Me too."

While Joe and his grandpa were exploring the area, Alice was at home relaxing with her mother. Alice had told Miss Jesse that they would talk more later but when she saw Miss Jesse approaching in her car, she was still surprised. Alice would rather spend the rest of the afternoon with her mother, but Miss Jesse was there and she was getting out of her car.

"Hello, Alice," Miss Jesse Mae said. "How are you doing today?"

"I'm fine. How about you?" said Alice. "Come on up and have a seat."

Miss Jesse Mae walked up onto the porch and sat down beside Alice. "I hear that you are leaving tomorrow," she said.

"Yeah," Alice replied. "We will be on that six thirty train."

"Have you found out anything that would keep Josh from returning to Swamp Town?"

"Not a thing. I went by to see Sarah then we took Joe to see his great grandma. We asked a lot of questions and no one knew of anyone or any reason why Josh could not return to Swamp Town. Grandma Williams suggested that she and I go to the courthouse and ask if there were any charges against Josh for any reason. The clerk said that everything was just fine so Josh and I will talk it over and see what we can do. Hopefully, we will be able to come back home. Mrs. Williams said that she already knew what they would say. She just wanted me to hear it for myself. I felt real good about that and I can give the official information to Josh."

"I hope everything works out. It would be nice if you two moved back here," said Miss. Jesse Mae and then stood up. "I hope to see you both soon." As she drove away, she gave a good-bye toot on her horn.

Alice had returned to her state of relaxation. Her mother was in the kitchen preparing dinner for the family and Grandpa and Joe had not returned from their exploratory trip on the farm. It was a bright sunny day and nothing seemed to be moving except when she looked in the direction of Miss Sarah's house. There she saw a cloud of dust moving on the path from the big house to the road that passed Alice's family house and the car leading the dust cloud was being driven by Brenda. When Brenda got to where Alice sat, she drove into the yard.

"Hello, Alice," Brenda said. "How are you doing today?"

"I'm fine," said Alice. "Come on up and have a seat."

"Where is Joe?" Brenda asked.

"His grandpa took him out on the farm someplace. I guess they just wanted to get used to each other."

"That's a very good thing. When are you going back home?"

"I'm leaving tomorrow morning on the six thirty train."

"I'm going to Baton Rouge tomorrow morning. Can I give you a ride?"

"That would be just great, but we would have to leave early."

"I'll see you then," said Brenda. She backed out of the yard and headed down the road toward Jesse Mae's place.

When Grandpa and Joe arrived home that afternoon, Joe was very excited about all of the things that he and Grandpa had seen. He could hardly wait to tell his mother what his grandpa had shown him.

Grandma called her family to dinner. Joe followed his mother all the way to the table, telling her what they had seen. Alice's mother, Mavis, was very quiet for the rest of the day but after Alice lay down for the night, her mother came in and said to her, "Please try to encourage Josh to return to Swamp Town, I want my family here with me." I'd love to have my grandson around me, and I miss you, too."

"I'll do what I can," said Alice. "I'll do what I can."

The family was up early that Saturday morning, and they were all dressed and having breakfast when they heard a car horn blow. It was Brenda. She was there, just like she had said she would be and would be a sad departure for the Wilson family. Jake hugged his daughter and grandson in the kitchen but did not go to the front door. He could not bear to see her leave. Brenda and Joe helped to put the luggage in the trunk of the car while Alice and her mother hugged each other until Joe tugged at her arm and said it's time to go.

The first five miles of the trip to Baton Rouge was as quiet as it could be. The two ladies said not a word and Joe went back to sleep. Alice was the first to break the silence, "Why are you going to Baton Rouge this morning?" she asked.

"I have an interview for a job," Brenda told her. "And as you know, Betty and Joe are half brother and sister. I wanted to ask you if you would work with me in helping them to understand who they are in relation to each other. I feel so bad about what happened to Betty, and I don't want that to happen to anyone else. I know that my grandma meant no harm but what my father did was a crime, and she kept a secret that has created a world of trouble."

"I'll be glad to work with you and I'm so happy that you have told me how you feel," said Alice.

A few minutes later, Brenda parked the car in front of the train station. Alice and Joe got out of the car and walked around to the trunk to get their luggage. Brenda got out of the car and opened the trunk. By this time, the porter was there with the cart. He loaded the luggage on the cart and headed into the train station.

Alice said, "Thank you for the ride and if we can come back home, I would like to talk with you some more."

"I would like that," Brenda told Alice. "I'll see you when you get back."

Joe had walked to the counter with the porter. Alice went to the counter and presented their tickets then while the porter put their things on the train. Alice and Joe climbed aboard the train and relaxed for a long ride home. Joe had enjoyed his trip to the country. He had seen things of which he had never dreamed of.

The train was a bit late getting to the station in Chicago, but when they walked into the luggage pickup area, there sitting on a bench was Josh. At first glance, Joe streamed out his name and ran straight for him. Josh had borrowed his friend's car and was waiting to take his family home. A porter was standing next to Josh and Alice, waiting for them to point their luggage out so he could take it to their car.

Joe pointed to a suitcase on a cart and said, "Look over there, Dad. There is one of our bags."

Josh said, "Yeah, Joseph, that is one of our bags all right."

The porter walked over and picked up the bag then asked, "Did you call him Joseph?"

"Yes, I did," said Josh.

"I thought that I recognized you," said the porter.

"Yes, yes. You are the man who helped me the first time I came to Chicago. That young man is named after you." Josh said with pride and appreciation in his heart.

"Well, well, I have someone who is named after me. It makes me feel good." He then took the bags out to the cart and put them in the trunk of the car. When he left to go back into the station, he turned to Joe and said, "Good-bye, Mr. Joseph.

"How did things go in Swamp Town?" Josh asked Alice.

"Very good," said Alice. "We'll have a lot to talk about tomorrow, but now all I want is some sleep."

CHAPTER 17

THE NEXT MORNING, Josh got up early and quietly. He wanted Alice to sleep in because he knew that her trip had been tiring so he went to the kitchen and started preparing breakfast. When Joe heard him moving around, he got up and joined him. Joe was wide awake and ready to talk to his father about his trip to Swamp Town.

"Daddy, Daddy," Joe called out as he entered the kitchen. "Guess what Grandpa did…he took me for a long, long walk. We saw a snake and frogs and lots of birds. We saw a large golden spider web, and there was a big rice field that was filled with water."

"Did you enjoy it?" asked Josh.

"Yes, yes," Joe replied. "I also enjoyed Grandma Sarah, Grandma Williams, and my sister Betty. Then we went down the dirt road and talked to Miss Jesse Mae."

"You sound like you enjoyed yourself."

That morning, Josh had prepared grits, fried eggs, and scrapple with a nice hot cup of coffee for his wife. Joe was still talking about his trip. Now it was about the things that he saw from the window of the train. His mother must have heard him or maybe it was the aroma of the food. Whatever it was, it brought her into the kitchen.

Alice sat down at the kitchen table and said, "What's all this noise about?

"It's about all of that fun you two had in Swamp Town," Josh told her.

"Yeah, Mom. Tell him all about the fun we had in Swamp Town," said Joe.

"I would rather find out about what went on in Swamp Town," said Josh. He needed to find out if he could go back to Swamp Town with a reasonable amount of safety.

"I took Joe by to see his grandma Sarah and told her why I was in town...that you were sick and that the doctor suggested that you leave the cold weather and all of those chemicals at the stockyard and that she said that you may be better off living down there in the warmer climate. Your mother said that she believed that your grandmother wanted you to come home and that there was no charge against you. Miss Sarah suggested that we go over to your grandmother's house and talk with her, so we went to your grandmother's house and spoke to her, Marge, and Brenda. Not one of them spoke against you. Then Mrs. Williams asked me to go to the courthouse with her. We went there and ask for the record of the death of the two people who drowned in the creek near Swamp Town on the date in question. The clerk gave Mrs. Williams a copy of the court's record that did not mention you in any way. "On our way home that afternoon, Mrs. Williams gave a copy of the court's record to me and said 'this is for you.' Then she said that she already knew that he was innocent because the sheriff told her so a long time ago. Your grandmother wanted me to see for myself that you were not charged."

"Well, it looks like you have done a good job of checking things out," Josh told her.

"We also went down to Miss Jesse Mae's place and talked to her and she says that she has not heard any negative talk about you," Alice said.

"This gives me a lot to think about. Let me take a few days, then we'll talk again."

The following week, nothing was said about the trip to Swamp Town. They continued their work without speaking to anyone about what may or may not happen. That Saturday, after the week was over, Josh spoke of a coughing attack that had occurred the previous Wednesday on his way to work. "I wanted to hold off until this weekend to talk to you. I think that we ought to try Swamp Town out and see how it works," he told her. "What do you think?"

"Let's give it a try," said Alice. "I don't want to lose you. I don't know what I'd do without you." She tried to hold back the tears.

"What about work? Do you think that we'll be able to find any work down there?"

"Don't worry, we'll find something to do."

The first thing that Monday morning, they both reported to their supervisors and gave notice that they were resigning in two weeks and a note was sent to Joe's school, saying that he would be moving to another school and requested that he be transferred. That Monday morning, Alice sent her parents a telegram stating that they would be moving back to Swamp Town in about two weeks.

Before they left, Josh took Alice and Joseph to Mary's place to say good-bye to his friends. The day they got on the train, it was Joseph, Josh's friend, the porter who loaded his bags on the train. They said their last good-byes on the platform before boarding the train.

Alice's mother received the telegram at seven o'clock that Tuesday evening. It read, "We'll be home the first of next month."

Mrs. Wilson went immediately to Sarah's house, but she was still working. Mavis went to the big house kitchen where she knew Sarah would be. Sarah was filled with Joy when she read that Josh and Alice were coming home at the beginning of the next month. Marge heard the excitement and came to the kitchen door.

"They are coming home," Sarah said. :They are coming home. My boy is coming home." The tears were flowing from their eyes. Sarah sat at the table, this time with the tears of joy.

"I'll go tell Mrs. Williams," Marge said. "She'll be glad to hear this."

Marge told Mrs. Williams who immediately got up and went into the kitchen to be with the other ladies. She joined Sarah at the table, the both of them, crying with tears of joy.

"Thank God. I have prayed for this for a long time, you know," Mrs. Williams said to the other women in the kitchen. "He, Betty, and Brenda are the only people in my bloodline." She spoke as if she was talking to herself. "I want to thank you, Mavis, for letting us know what's going on, and Sarah, I'm so glad that you are such a good person. Thanks for everything you do."

Sarah knew that Mrs. Williams was truly thankful and that she wanted Josh back in her life. This made Sarah feel good. She smiled and said, "Thank you."

Marge had sat there with a smile on her face. She had remained in the big house because of her love for Mrs. Williams but now that Josh is coming back. She can go back to the coast and be with her family, and Brenda will be able to visit her child anytime she visits her grandma.

Mrs. Williams turned to Marge and said, "Marge, if Josh will accept it, I'm going to ask him to oversee the property and you will be welcome to remain here as long as you like."

"Thank you," said Marge. "I'll stay here long enough to teach him the paperwork then I'll move back to the coast to be with my family."

"I appreciate that," Mrs. Williams told her. "We'll talk more later." Then she turned to Sarah and said, "When Josh gets here, I want to meet with him and Marge as soon as possible."

Before Alice and her family left Chicago, she wrote a letter to her father, asking him to pick them up from the train station. The ride home was quiet. Joe was looking out the window and Alice was relaxed in Josh's arms, sleeping most of the time. Josh had a jittery feeling, wondering if he was doing the right thing, where would he get work and how long would it take him to get a place to live. When they got off the train, Alice's father was at the station, waiting for the train.

Joe was the first to see his grandpa and ran to greet him. Grandpa picked Joe up, hugging tightly and reached out for his daughter and son-in-law. Mr. Wilson told Josh that he was going to live with him until he found a place to live.

"Thank you," Josh said. Then he asked, "Will you take me by Mama's house so I can speak to her? You know, I've not seen her for a long time."

"Okay," said Mr. Wilson. "We'll drop you off. You visit your mama and get some sleep, then you can unload your thing tomorrow morning."

It was twelve midnight when Josh knocked on his mother's door. She was wide awake in anticipation of his arrival. She grabbed her son, hugged him and the tears fell from both of their eyes. It was a quiet time now. Her eyes searched his face and soul, trying to find out what was wrong with her son and if there was anything that she could do to make it better.

"How is that cough, Josh? Is it any better?" she asked. "What are you taking for it?"

"It comes in spells, Mama. We'll know more about how I'm doing after I've been down here for a while."

"Well," said his mother. "You'd better get some sleep, your grandma Williams wants to have a meeting with you and Marge tomorrow morning."

Josh was awakened the following morning by the aroma of his favorite breakfast coming from the kitchen. For him, his mother had prepared—smoked ham and eggs with cheese biscuits and molasses. It was early but Josh wanted to get up and have breakfast with his mother, then he would go over to his father-in-law's house and take the luggage out of the trunk of the car. They sat there for a while enjoying a good breakfast and in reminiscence of times gone by.

When Josh left the house, he asked his mother to give him a call when the Williamses were ready for the meeting.

"Okay," said his mother. "Now you get over here as soon as you can."

As Josh walked down the path that lead to the main road of Swamp Town, the fog hung low as it always did. The sun had just begun to show its orange glow above the horizon and Josh could see the smoke coming out of the chimney of the Wilson's kitchen. Mrs. Wilson was already up and getting breakfast for the family.

Josh knocked on the front door.

Alice opened the door and said, "Hello, early bird. Why are you up so early?"

"I'm here to take the bags out of the car," Josh told her.

Alice's older brother was now in the military so Mrs. Wilson gave his room to Alice and Josh; Joe would be sleeping on the sofa. The Wilsons were getting ready for breakfast, while Josh, who had eaten at his mother's house, went out on the porch and sat down in the cool morning breeze. He was trying to figure out where to start looking for a job. At that point, he heard a voice from the kitchen.

It was Alice saying, "Josh, pick up the phone."

"I got it," he said, then he got up, went into the house, and answered the phone.

It was Sarah who said, "The Williams wants to know if you can come over here now."

"I'll be there in twenty minutes," Josh said. He was a bit nervous, not knowing what it was all about. He dressed neatly but casually and walked over to the Williams's house, thinking along the way that he was invited and wondered if he should go to the front door or through the kitchen where his mother was working. *I'll go through the kitchen,* he thought *and walked up to the kitchen door and knocked gently.*

"Come in, they are waiting for you." Sarah walked Josh to the parlor door and said, "Josh is here."

"Come in," said Mrs. Williams. "and Sarah, I want you to join us also." When Josh walked in, Mrs. Williams reached out and gave her grandson a big hug. "I'm so glad to see you, son, and I'm so sorry for the harm and hurt that I've cause you. Will you forgive me?"

"Yes, Yes," said Josh, "Everything is going to be all right." Sarah and Josh walked over and sat on the sofa facing Marge, who had some papers in front of her.

"By the way, how are you doing Josh, did you have a nice trip," Mrs. Williams asked.

"I still have a few problems with the coughing spells but it's better when I take my medicine," he told her. "And the trip was just fine."

"Good morning, Josh," Marge said. "Are you ready to get down to business."

"I'm as ready as I can be," Josh replied.

Mrs. Williams sat in a chair on the other side of the room, facing the three of them. Josh, she said, "I'm glad that you are back home, and I know that you are going to be needing a job. The reason I wanted to see you first thing this morning is because I have a job and I wanted to offer it to you before you start looking somewhere else. I want you to become the overseer of my property. Now Marge has been doing the administrative work, but she has plans to return to the gulf so that she can be with her family. I want you to take over the entire job which includes checking the crops, purchasing the seeds, supplies and the necessary equipment and keeping records. Marge has promised to remain here for three months. She and I will instruct you in all of the things that you need to know. If you accept this job, we start work on Monday morning. What do you say?"

"I have an easy answer for that question, and it is yes," Josh told her. "I'm very happy for the offer and I'll do a good job for you. Thank you very much." Josh was trying to be very business-like but his heart was beating like a drum in his chest.

"We'll meet here, starting at nine o'clock Monday morning," Mrs. Williams told them.

Josh left the Williams's house and walked back to find his wife busy putting their things in a small closet that was built for one person. He knew that it would not be like that for long, so he took his wife's hand and told her that Mrs. Williams had just given him a job. She streamed with delight, bringing her parents to the door to find out what was going on.

Alice grabbed her mother around the neck and said, "He has got a job. My Josh has got a job."

That Monday morning, Alice walked Betty and Joe to school. She had to get Joe registered and since she had to go to the school with Josh, she took Betty along with her. The school had grown considerably with more rooms and several additional teachers. She took Betty to her classroom and Joe to the office and had him registered. On her way out of the school, she heard the voice of Mr. Smith and decided to see if it was really him. Mr. Smith recognized her as she passed his open door and excused himself from his class and walked over to speak with her.

She spoke with him about Josh's new job and that they had moved back to Swamp Town. She also told him that she was at the school to register her son.

Mr. Smith congratulated her and told her how happy he was to see her, then he went to his desk and wrote a note and gave it to Alice and said, "Give this to Josh."

"I will," Alice told him.

Mrs. Williams and Marge had taken Josh around the property to introduce him to the tenants as the overseer. They also took him around the perimeter of the property so that he could get to see the boundary of the entire place.

Alice had read the note from Mr. Smith and could hardly wait for Josh to get home. Mrs. Williams and Marge dropped Josh off at the Wilson's house at about two o'clock that afternoon.

Alice met Josh at the door and asked, "How did your day go?" Did you cough any today?"

"Just fine," he said. "She put me on the payroll today."

"Oh, thank God!" Alice said. "You must have done something right." Then she gave him the note from Mr. Smith. It reads, "Contact Mr. Johnson at the parish trade school. They have a class in agriculture there."

"You are right, honey," Josh replied. "Someone is taking care of me. I'll ask your father if I can use his car to check the school out tomorrow after I'm finished with my work with the Williams."

That Tuesday, Marge introduced Josh to all the paperwork involved in the business of running a farm. This session was the primary introduction, there would be much more to follow. Josh spoke to Mrs. Williams, his grandma, about going to check out the class on agriculture. Saying that Mr. Smith had talked to Alice and thought that class could help him. She was excited, because he was already interested in learning how to better himself, "I'm glad that you are showing a lot of interest and I believe that class will help you out a great deal. By all means, go to the class and take the course. That will be part of the job and you may use my car." At first, Josh didn't think that he should tell her about the class. Now he was very happy that he did; going to this class will be part of his job.

The school was about ten miles from Swamp Town. Josh decided to use Mrs. Williams's car to check out the school, so he stopped by to tell Alice which car he was going to use, then headed to the Parish Vocational school to sign up for the class.

He started his school class that following Monday and continued his instruction by Marge and Mrs. Williams for the next three months. He was free then to take charge of his overseer's position but still had three additional months to complete his class at the Parish Vocational School. After completing his classes, Josh and Alice moved into the house that his friend Jack's family had vacated.

Brenda was now settled in her teaching job in Baton Rouge and was able to spend her weekends with her grandmother and Betty. Mrs. Williams was rid of her responsibilities of overseeing the property and had ample time to work in her flower garden, and Josh had now purchased himself a car, making Mrs. Williams's car available for her to go on long drives in the beautiful countryside around Lake Pontchartrain. The move of hiring Josh to be the overseer of the property had taken a lot of pressure off Mrs. Williams. She could now move around among friends, enjoying life. She often visit Brenda in Baton Rouge for dinner and shopping, knowing every month Josh would bring the books to her for inspection.

It was Sunday afternoon, Josh and Alice was sitting on their front porch relaxing when Alice asked, "Have you had a coughing spell lately?"

"No," said Josh. "And I have not even thought about it and I have not been cold either."

"That sounds good," Alice said. "Let's hope it stays that way."

Sarah and Josh had noticed that Mrs. Williams had been spending a lot of time in Baton Rouge lately. Sometimes, Brenda would bring her home in the middle of the week and then take her back for the weekend. They had not however noticed that she had been losing weight. Lately, however, Brenda spent the night with her, and the following morning, she came to the kitchen and told Sarah that her grandmother was ill and that they had been going to the doctor and taking care of some business. She did not say what the illness was nor did Sarah asked. Brenda called her brother, Josh, that afternoon and asked him to come to the big house.

Josh and Alice showed up at the big house at five o'clock wondering what Mrs. Williams wanted.

Mrs. Williams said to Josh, "I'm going to spend some time with Brenda in Baton Rouge, so I want you to take the key to the safe and put all of your record there. I'll see them when I get back. You continue what you are doing, and the banker will continue to mail you your check."

"I'll do that," Josh told her. It was at that point that Josh knew that something was very wrong.

Brenda had grown up and loved her grandma very much and it was very obvious that she was taking her home to give her the best care that she could get. It was two months later that Josh got a call from Brenda, who said that their grandmother wanted to come home and needed a nurse to help take care of her, and that she would contact the nurse. She would have the nurses to come and prepare the place for her grandmother's comfort. She also told Josh that their grandmother has written a letter of authority for him to pay for whatever she needs. Brenda made sure that everyone understood that she would be coming home to be with her grandma for as much as she could.

The next morning, Sarah went out to Mrs. Williams's garden and picked some of her favorite flowers and placed them in her room. On Sarah's face, a person could see the hurt that she bore in her heart when she saw the nurse come in and prepared a place for the comfort of her friend. Betty was at her side and Sarah could see in her eyes that she could feel that something was wrong. They brought Mrs. Williams home and placed her by a window where she could see her beautiful flowers. It was there that they found her a week later.

After the funeral, Josh found himself depressed because he had no idea what he was going to do. How would he take care of his family now? Would he have to go back and live in that room at his father-in-law's house? And what would his mother do? He had quite a problem but he was told to keep doing his job until he was told to stop and that's what he was going do.

That following Monday, Brenda called and asked Josh if he would come to Baton Rouge on Wednesday morning at nine o'clock. When he got to Brenda's apartment, she was waiting for him. She hopped into his car and told him the address to go to. They went to Mrs. Williams's attorney's office. On their way there, she told him that the will would be read.

"Who else will be there?" Josh asked.

"Mama's supposed to be here, but she said that she would not be able to make it," Brenda told him.

"Why am I here?" Josh asked.

"Because you, Betty, and I are her only descendants."

Josh and Brenda walked the flight of stairs to the attorney's office.

"Come in," the attorney said. "This won't take long. Your grandmother had been seeing me on and off for some time now. She had been ill for a long time and wanted to get things straight before she left. So all I have to do is read it."

To Marge, she leaves fifty thousand dollars.

To Brenda, her granddaughter, she leaves one hundred fifty thousand dollars and the homesite.

To Josh, she leaves the remainder of the property and one hundred thousand dollars.

On their way back to Brenda's place, she asked Josh if he would keep the grave site clean.

"I'll do that," said Josh. "I'll be glad to do that."

When Josh got home that afternoon, Alice asked, "What are we going to do, Josh?"

Josh said, "My grandmother must have suffered a great deal these last days. She must have cried a lot, knowing that her son was a rapist, losing her son and his father, and having a second grandchild with the problems of someone born of incest that she could have prevented if she had just told us that we were siblings. I believe that she put me in her will in an attempt to make up for some of the things that she believed that she could have avoided, so she left me with some funds and some money to run the place with. Because she put me in her will, we'll be okay."